"What?" Isaac watched as the woman he'd just proposed to ran away as if she chased after something precious.

He'd seen the eyes whose sparkle teased him his entire life awash with tears of joy. Everyone knew Nessa wanted to be his wife—Nessa herself had made sure of it. So why did she flee what she claimed to have wanted so badly?

Nothing is sure when it comes to women. Michael's words from earlier that day rose to his thoughts.

Fair enough, Isaac allowed. But it wasn't unreasonable to assume that the woman who had been all but a man's betrothed since the cradle should accept his proposal. Really, asking the question itself was more a formality than anything else.

To think he'd wasted so much thought and time in preparing his proposal! He kicked the stone upon which she'd sat, dislodging smaller pieces to rain on the grass beneath. How dare she refuse him? Nessa had led him on for years only to reject him when he came to the sticking point? Unbelievable!

He strode through the woods, breaths coming fast and shallow as he stomped away from the site of his humiliation. Nessa was *his* by rights. Her willingness to be his bride was owed him. How could she turn her back on him as though his offer was hardly worth the breath it took her to refuse?

Lord, I pushed aside my own desires to shoulder my responsibility to Nessa and our families. I longed to choose my own wife, lay the path I'd follow, but knew it wasn't my place to flout the plan You had for me. I bowed to what I believed to be Your will. How could I make such a mistake?

KELLY EILEEN HAKE

In the six years since Kelly Eileen Hake received her first writing contract, she's continued writing fiction from short stories to novels. During the same period of time, Kelly earned her BA in Literature and her credential to teach English. Currently she is working toward her MA in Writing Popular Fiction.

Books by Kelly Eileen Hake

HEARTSONG PRESENTS

Don't miss out on any of our super romances. Write to us at the following address for information on our newest releases and club information.

Heartsong Presents Readers' Service
PO Box 721
Uhrichsville, OH 44683

Or visit www.heartsongpresents.com

A Time
to Laugh

Kelly Eileen Hake

Heartsong Presents

This is dedicated to Julia Rich, my reader and support system as I wrote this book. And, as always, thanks to the wonderful team at Barbour and to our Lord who oversees the work.

A note from the Author:
I love to hear from my readers! You may correspond with me by writing:

Kelly Eileen Hake
Author Relations
PO Box 721
Uhrichsville, OH 44683

ISBN 978-1-59789-934-5

A TIME TO LAUGH

Our mission is to publish and distribute inspirational products offering exceptional value and biblical encouragement to the masses.

PRINTED IN THE U.S.A.

one

Saddleback, Montana, 1916

"You can't catch me!" Isaac Freimont stuck his thumbs in his ears, waggling his fingers at Nessa Gailbraith as she flew toward him from across the meadow. When she got too close for comfort, he took off again.

"That does it, Isaac!" Nessa puffed the words as she shot after him. "Those were my best stockings, and you've ruined them!" She picked up a burst of speed and grabbed the tail of his shirt as it flapped behind him.

"Okay, okay." Caught, he put his hands up in mock surrender. "I promise I'll never again use your stockings to catch tadpoles."

His earnest blue eyes made Nessa grudgingly relinquish her grip on his shirt.

"Unless you take them off to dip your feet in the pond and leave them under my nose!" With that, he sprung away like a hare eluding a wolf.

"Isaac Freimont, you come back here!" Nessa hollered as she took up the chase once more, glorying in the feel of the soft spring grass between her toes. Nothing could be better than playing with her best friend in the warm sunshine. "You know I'll get you sooner or later!"

Vanessa Gailbraith's fond smile at the memory wavered as she considered that last line, uttered with all the brash confidence of youth. How disappointed her eight-year-old self would have been to know that it would be later rather than sooner. A full decade later, and she still chased after Isaac

5

Freimont in a thrilling mixture of excitement and frustration.

And Isaac still runs like the wind. Nessa grimaced ruefully. No matter how much she felt ready for marriage, Isaac's stubbornness outstripped hers. She'd sent more prayers to heaven than she could count, but it seemed the Lord's will aligned with Isaac's so far. But Nessa's prayers brought a new sense of peace of late. Soon things would change. . . .

"Nessa"—Julia's voice nabbed her attention—"you've got that look again."

"What look?" Nessa widened her eyes at her best friend.

"The one that means you've hatched another scheme to make Isaac notice you." Julia shook her head. "The one that means you'll try to elicit my help. The look," she finished triumphantly, "that always comes before a lot of trouble."

"I've no idea what you mean." Nessa shrugged off Julia's concerns. "Though I was thinking that a new hairstyle might be in order, as it's becoming so hot."

"That's true enough," Julia agreed as she gazed at the expanse of blue overhead. "Not a cloud in sight nor whisper of a breeze. Wait." Her eyes narrowed in suspicion. "What kind of hairstyle were you thinking of, Nessa?"

"It's so thick and heavy it's always escaping my pins." Nessa reached up to finger a burnished mahogany strand. "And then it frizzes something awful around my face. I despair of looking like a proper lady whenever I catch a glimpse of myself in the mirror over the washstand." She heaved a woeful sigh.

"And there's nothing more to it than that?" Julia quirked an eyebrow. "Because every single other time you've altered your appearance—or tried to, at least—it's been in hopes of attracting Isaac's notice. To my recollection, none of those endeavors ended well at all. *Disastrous* is more the word."

"I'm sure I don't know what you mean." Nessa tilted her chin toward the sky. "Every young lady tries to look her best, with some efforts making better progress than others."

"Then I suppose you're about due for something to work," Julia teased. "Seeing as how everything else failed so badly!"

"Now that's not true, and you know it!"

"Oh, I know it *is* true. I remember the time you ordered that special face scrub and walked around looking as though you'd been boiled." Julia bit her lip to keep from laughing.

"Pumice was supposed to reveal a natural glow," Nessa defended indignantly before giving in to a small smile of her own. "Though I did shine like a lantern until Dr. Bunting's Sunburn Remedy arrived. At any rate, this is nothing like that. I just want you to give my hair a little trim."

"Me?" Her best friend leaned back. "I've never cut your hair before. Why on earth would you put the shears in my hand?"

"You cut your little brothers' hair, and they always look nice. Hair is hair, so I would think you'd be able to manage."

"I don't know. Kyle's and Leon's hair are a lot straighter than yours." Julia eyed Nessa's thick, curly locks with obvious trepidation. "And it's harder to mess up when it's supposed to be short. A woman's hair is her crowning glory, Nessa!"

"No, your hair is your crowning glory." Nessa gestured at her friend's sleek blonde bun. "Mine resembles a dandelion. . .all fluffed and scattered." She smoothed the springy tendrils creeping away from her pins. "Since these curls won't stay down, I thought we could try trimming them so they twist around my face instead of whipping in the wind. It's the newest fashion—how hard can it be? I have a copy of *McCall's* magazine at home to show you what I mean. Will you help me?"

"I'll do my best," Julia agreed. "But I can't promise it will turn out the way you want it."

"That's fine." Nessa cast a glance toward the direction of the Freimont homestead. *I'm used to things not turning out the way I'd hoped.*

≈

"Hopes aren't promises." Isaac Freimont mixed the oats, linseed, and old milk to slop the hogs. The thick mixture oozed into the trough as he waited for his father's response.

"And the best laid plans are not guaranteed to be followed," Pa rejoined. "Arthur, Jakob, and I were to have an entire extra year before the womenfolk arrived. We'd hoped to have a home built and a farm running by that time."

"But Ma came early and brought with her everything from windows to trees." Isaac grinned as he finished the familiar story. His parents had a difficult start in the Montana wilderness, but they'd prospered through hard work and love.

"Your ma brought a sight more than wagonloads of goods, son."

"I know. . . . She brought along the Bannings and Grandma Albright and her little brother, Isaac. When he left to go be a miner, she named me after him."

"She certainly did. There's family history in your name, and we both thought it fit, seeing as how you surprised us coming so many years after your sister. But I wasn't talking about that. When your ma made the journey to Montana, she carried determination, love, and faith that through God we could build a home—and a family—together." Dustin Freimont straightened from where he'd been reinforcing the pigpen. "I pray that someday you'll have a helpmeet who brings you such joy. We've long thought your friendship with Nessa would turn to something deeper, but you know your own mind."

"I do care for Nessa." Isaac put down the slop bucket. "She's been one of my closest friends since we were toddlers."

"Sure surprised your ma and me when we discovered your ma was pregnant with you sixteen years after Marlene. Your ma and Rosalind Maclean never expected to bear children within a month of one another." Pa headed for the barn. "Seemed like a God-given blessing that you and Nessa had each other before the railroad brought new folks and children of their own."

"We've gained steady friends in the Horntons," Isaac agreed. "But it can't be forgotten that our family and the MacLeans founded Saddleback. This land is precious as blood to me, Julia, Nessa. . .all of us."

"Still another thing you and Nessa share." Pa spoke lightly, but Isaac knew that the conversation had been steered back to its original purpose.

"Yes." He bit back a heavy sigh as he grabbed a currycomb and began to brush Goliath—the biggest horse in town. Possibly the biggest horse in all Montana, for that matter. "You, Ma, and practically everyone else in Saddleback have been dropping hints that it's time I spoke for Nessa."

"You understand we're not trying to pressure you?" Pa gave a wry grin. "Well, most of us aren't. We want to know your intentions. Nessa is a beautiful girl who will make some man a wonderful wife. But so long as there's the conception that you two have an understanding, the other men in town maintain more of a distance. It's come to the point where you need to prove up on your claim or move on, son."

At the not-so-subtle reminder that Isaac was of an age to be establishing his own spread and acquiring a wife to work alongside him, Isaac's jaw clenched. Why were land and women used to take the measure of a man?

"It's not fair to Nessa to string her along if you don't believe she's the woman for you." Pa prodded him to respond after a stretch of silence. "That doesn't mean you can't let her loose and pursue the gal who's caught your eye."

"Subtle, Pa." Isaac shook his head. "No one's caught my eye, as you put it. Nessa's the best girl I'll ever meet."

"Then why do you hesitate?"

How could a man tell his father he chafed at having his entire life decided for him? That Isaac Freimont often wished he could follow his Uncle Isaac Albright's example and make his own way? Instead, everyone took for granted that he'd stay in town—a dutiful son—and marry Nessa as they expected.

"When a path has been laid before you," Isaac struggled to explain, "everyone assumes you'll take it. Saddleback will always be my home, and Nessa has always been the girl by my side. It seems the path heads straight down the aisle." He swallowed hard. "But you understand that a man has to make his own way. If I marry Nessa, when have I stood on my own?"

two

Alone in front of the looking glass, her eyes closed, Nessa wondered if she'd made the right choice. Cracking open a single eyelid, she spied the curls strewn about the floor and squeezed her eyes shut again in a hurry.

"I'm back." Julia's voice sounded from the doorway. "I snagged Da's shaving brush so I can sweep the bits off your neck." With that, a ticklish stroke caught Nessa behind the ear.

"Oh," she gasped, eyes flying open as she giggled at the sensation. The mirth faded as she stared at her reflection. Biting her lip, Nessa turned her head from one side to the other, silently appraising her new hairstyle from every angle.

"Well?" Julia stood behind her, hands clasped tightly.

"I love it!" Her reddish brown locks retained most of their original length but boasted fashionable curls framing her face and resting gently at the nape of her neck. "Even better than I'd hoped! But"—she sobered as she considered—"I've liked things and have been proven wrong before. What do *you* think?"

"Well, not that I'm completely impartial, but I'd say it's charming. Those little curls add softness to your face and make your eyes seem brighter." Her friend couldn't resist teasing her. "How does it feel to have one of your plans actually work?"

"Ha, ha." Nessa deadpanned but couldn't keep her smile at bay for long. The springy tendrils made her eyes seem bigger, drawing attention away from a jaw a hint too strong for beauty and a mouth too wide for ladylike poise. "It's. . .nice."

"I should say so." Julia whisked the hair on the floor into a dustpan. "Hmm. . .I'd say there's just enough for a dolly for Meagan." She transferred the wisps to her palm and held it up for Nessa's inspection. "Though you'd have to sew on the hair. I've no skill for such detailed work."

"You always think of others." Nessa gave her friend a hug. "And I'd be glad to make your little sister a dolly." When she drew back from the hug, she cocked her head to one side.

"Nessa Gailbraith, are you trying to see your reflection even now?" Julia shook her head. "Vanity is a sin, you know."

"How could I know such a thing when I've never before looked half as good as I do now?" Nessa batted her lashes playfully. "But, no, I wasn't looking into the mirror. I was thinking how odd it is that the one thing I'm more skilled at than you is the last thing anyone would ever suspect."

"Your sewing, you mean?" Julia tucked the hair into a small box. "Mine is serviceable and solid, but you have a way with a needle fit to make thread dance into place. And others know it well. Why would you think your talent an unlikely one?"

"Simply because it requires long periods of sitting still and paying attention to exacting detail." Nessa shrugged. "I surprise even myself that I've the patience for such work. You must admit, I've precious little patience in other matters."

"True. And yet you've waited long years for Isaac to declare his love." Julia tweaked one curl. "With time and happiness, you'll settle well into the role of wife and mother."

"How is it you always say exactly the right thing. . .and somehow sound like a wise old woman when you're scarcely a month older than I am? At times I'm sure God intended our friendship since I so lack your wisdom and discernment."

"And your joy and enthusiasm make life more exciting." Julia gave her a swift hug. "Now that your hair is done, when will you contrive to show Isaac your new glamour?"

"You make it sound as though I went out to California and visited Max Factor's studio. Glamour," Nessa scoffed. "Oh, wait. Did I tell you I'd ordered pressed face powder?"

"You didn't!" Julia's pretty blue eyes grew round. "I know it's in fashion, but what place is there for such airs in Montana? Besides, if Nancy Rutgers were to ever catch on to it, she'd denounce you as a loose woman!"

"Oh, Nancy is a stiff-necked matron, to be sure." Nessa set her jaw. "But there is no shame in powder, Julia. I'm not rouging my lips or painting my nails, after all. Powder bears no scandal—especially if no one knows of it."

"How do you always make your plans sound perfectly reasonable even when I know there's something amiss?" Julia frowned and gave Nessa a critical glance. "Besides, your complexion is fine on its own. Why use artifice?"

"I overheard Isaac say he thought freckles to be a sure sign of wildness in a girl." Nessa bowed her head. "And I can never seem to resist tearing off my bonnet when there's no one about to see. So here I have these little spots on my nose."

"Your freckles are just as charming as your new hairstyle," Julia declared. "And Isaac is foolish to say aught against freckles when there are girls like Marcy Adams who were born with them and it doesn't mean she goes without her bonnet."

"Marcy Adams *is* beautiful," Nessa conceded. "But everyone knows the cause of my freckles. A swipe of powder will serve to lessen them, that's all. No one need know."

"I'll never speak enough sense to make you heed me." Julia smiled fondly. "You were always one to defy expectation."

❧

"Expectation." Isaac ground the word through gritted teeth as he stabbed his pitchfork into the hayloft. "The force standing against the free will God saw fit to grant us. Bane of a man's life."

"What is?" Michael's voice had Isaac peering over the edge of the hayloft before he swung a pitchfork load of hay onto his friend's head.

"Hello, Michael." Isaac waited until the other man started up the ladder before he continued feeding the horses. "Good thing I didn't pitch hay all over before I knew you were here."

"Why do you think I asked the question?" Michael's head popped over the top of the ladder. "I figured you didn't know I'd shown up, or you wouldn't waste time talking to yourself."

"And why wouldn't I?" Isaac tossed a pitchfork, and Michael easily caught it. "I'll have you know I'm good company."

"Poor fellow." Michael shrugged. "You know somethin' is weighin' heavy on a man's mind when he talks to himself and claims to enjoy the conversation. Now what was it you were calling the 'bane of a man's life?'"

"What do you think?" Isaac raised his brows.

"On a rough guess, I'd have to say. . .women?"

"Close enough," Isaac snorted. "The expectations of women are stifling our God-given free wills to the point where some men can't even see it happening anymore."

"Knowin' you as well as I do"—Michael leaned on his pitchfork and speculated—"I'd think this had something to do with Nessa."

"Pa cornered me earlier today to have a discussion," Isaac grimly acknowledged. "Said time's come when I need to claim her or cut her loose so someone else can speak up."

"Ah." Michael tilted his head. "Can't say you didn't see this comin'. Have you made your decision yet, or is that what all the grumbling was about when I walked in?"

"What do you think?" Isaac flung another forkful of hay over the side of the loft. "If I'd made my decision, there'd be no need to talk about it—even with myself."

"Have you talked to God about it?" Michael's simple question pulled Isaac up short. "And I don't mean in the past, either."

"I've prayed about it for a long time," Isaac admitted, "but didn't seek the Lord's wisdom after my talk with Pa. Don't know what I was thinking." *No wonder I've got no peace!*

"I'm going to go grab a drink of water. Maybe you ought to rectify your oversight while I'm gone, and we can talk about what decision you come to." With that, he hightailed it.

Lord, You know it rubs me the wrong way to have my bride chosen for me, but I'm ready to set up my own household. Pa's right that I need a helpmeet to do so, and wiser heads than my own have pointed me in Nessa's direction. Is that the answer?

"Well?" Michael, already back, had waited until Isaac opened his eyes again. "Any new insight?"

"Yeah." Isaac's grip tightened. "It's not Nessa who's the problem. It's me."

"Already knew that." His friend softened the words with a grin. "You don't like havin' the choice made for you—I understand that. Any man would. All the same, I think you're askin' yourself the wrong questions."

"How so?"

"You've been wondering whether or not you would feel right about marryin' Nessa—that's the way of it, yes?"

"Basically."

"That's as valid a question as any." Michael nodded. "But have you thought about the other side of the matter?"

"You mean wondering if Nessa wants to marry me?" Isaac's disbelief all but echoed in the rafters. "That's a given."

"Nothing about a woman is a sure bet," Michael shook a finger at his friend in warning. "And that's not what I meant. What I was wondering is if you thought about how you'd like it if you saw her marryin' some other guy when you moved on?"

"I'd be fi—" Something stopped Isaac from finishing his response. Nessa married to someone else? He threw down the pitchfork, causing little bits of hay to rise and tickle his nose. "She wouldn't," he evaded flatly.

"That didn't answer the question. You can't expect to not take her as your wife and have her pine away the rest of her life. We both know Nessa's got too much spirit for that."

"She's. . ." *Mine.* Isaac shook the thought from his head. He didn't own Nessa. "Free to do as she pleases, of course." The words caught in his craw, forcing him to retract them. "But I wouldn't like it." The thought of Nessa belonging to another man hadn't really hit him until that moment. "Not one bit."

"Now"—Michael rested his pitchfork against the wall— "*that's* an answer."

☙

Nessa clutched the handle of her bucket and hurried to the shady nook where she'd found an early batch of raspberries. Her family would enjoy them this evening with sweetened cream, and perhaps there would be enough left over to bake tarts the next morning. She might even save one for—

"Isaac!" She gasped and stepped backward as he burst from the trees to her left. "Oh, you gave me such a start! What are you doing here?"

"Hoped to find you." His response took her breath away.

"Well, here we are." Nessa raised a hand to straighten her

bonnet, only to realize she'd forgotten it yet again. Of all the times to be running about like a hoyden. . .

"Nessa," he stepped closer as he spoke, her name rumbling from deep in his chest, "there are things we need to speak of."

"Yes?" She didn't even try to hide the hopeful note of her voice as she gazed into his blue eyes. His hair shone golden in the sun's late rays. Hard to believe the scraggly friend of her childhood had grown into such a handsome man.

"Here." He cupped her elbow and led her to a flat rock shaded by a large tree. After he saw her comfortably seated, he straightened up to eye her thoughtfully. "You're looking well, Nessa."

"Thank you," she murmured, her fingers toying with one of her curls. This was it, the moment she'd prayed for, dreamed of—Isaac was going to go down on one knee and propose! He'd finally admit his deep love for her and beg her to be the wife at his side through the coming years. She gave a soft sigh.

"Now, Nessa," he stepped back a pace as he addressed her, "you know as well as I that all of Saddleback has been expecting us to wed for years now. We've a certain duty, if you will, to come through. Our families hope to be joined through our union."

"Certainly," she breathed. Here he was, speaking words of duty and responsibility. No wonder he'd distanced himself, so that when his proclamations of love came, he'd move close and take her in his arms. . . *Thank You, Lord!*

"Vanessa Gailbraith"—he stiffly knelt and took her hand in his—"will you stand before the town as my wife?"

"Oh—" The joyous "yes" died on her lips, a frown creasing her brow. Where was the declaration of love? The romantic vow that he could consider no other woman when she'd stood beside him for so long? The promise that he would cherish her as they joined their lives forever? He proposed as the suns rays set, but the beauty of the approaching night was lost to him.

"This must no longer be delayed." He'd obviously sensed her hesitation. "We cannot avoid the path laid before us, Nessa." His eyes pierced her with their intensity. "Let us bow to the inevitable and make the best of the bounty we've been given."

"The inevitable," she echoed faintly, clutching his hand so she wouldn't sway in her seat as his words hammered into the hopes of her heart. *Does he not love me, Lord?*

"Indeed." He nodded gravely. "We're of similar age, have known each other for all our lives. Our long-standing friendship shows we'll deal well enough together as man and wife."

"Well enough!" This time her echo bore more strength. How dare he ruin the moment she'd dreamed of for years with such rubbish as he now spoke. Her jaw clenched shut against the small part of her that whispered to accept his proposal and be content with whatever he offered.

"The timing is right for us to wed." He let go of her hand and rose to his feet.

"Oh?" She watched in fascination as her beloved began to pace before her, his hands tightening into fists as he moved back and forth.

Numbly, she wondered whether he was stalking reasons why they should marry, trying to capture them and convince himself it was the logical choice.

"The planting season is over with the harvest yet to begin. The weather is well enough, and the entire town will be able to attend the ceremony. It is an opportunity to engender the goodwill of all Saddleback—very important as we set about carving our place here."

"I see." She stared up at him, willing him to see what she

saw—that this travesty of a proposal didn't take into account all that they could build in their lifetime. To see their home, their children, their love as the treasure it could be. But no, he plowed on ahead with his speech.

"I knew you would. We're alike in that we understand the foundation of marriage really is—" He paused to give her a searching glance.

Her heart resumed its beat at the force of his gaze. Had he finally come to his senses? Would he cite the benefits of romance and tenderness?

"Hard work." His emphatic declaration doused her flicker of hope. "Raising a house, taming the land, and eking out a living all require backbreaking labor and determination. And I know better than anyone how hard you'll work alongside me, Nessa. What say we begin building that life now?"

"Isaac—" She choked on the words as he stood before her, proud of his reasons, certain in her response. Oblivious to her needs. "I—"

"Don't cry, Nessa." Isaac squatted beside her, running a work-roughened thumb over her cheek. "All you must do is say yes."

As she looked into the eyes of the man she'd loved so long, Nessa almost convinced herself to do it. He could recognize their love after their marriage, couldn't he? Isaac spoke of children, after all. And God had answered her prayers to be Isaac's wife. She took a gulp of air and prepared to agree.

"See, there's no need to be emotional."

His indulgent smile made her stomach lurch. "I—" Nessa stood, brushing away his hand. "I'm sorry, Isaac. I can't." Her tears made everything blend in a swirl of evening's darkness and her own despair. She pushed past him and ran as fast as her legs could carry her.

three

"What?" Isaac watched as the woman he'd just proposed to ran away as if she chased after something precious.

He'd seen the eyes whose sparkle teased him his entire life awash with tears of joy. Everyone knew Nessa wanted to be his wife—Nessa herself had made sure of it. So why did she flee what she claimed to have wanted so badly?

Nothing is sure when it comes to women. Michael's words from earlier that day rose to his thoughts.

Fair enough, Isaac allowed. But it wasn't unreasonable to assume that the woman who had been all but a man's betrothed since the cradle should accept his proposal. Really, asking the question itself was more a formality than anything else.

To think he'd wasted so much thought and time in preparing his proposal! He kicked the stone upon which she'd sat, dislodging smaller pieces to rain on the grass beneath. How dare she refuse him? Nessa had led him on for years only to reject him when he came to the sticking point? Unbelievable!

He strode through the woods, breaths coming fast and shallow as he stomped away from the site of his humiliation. Nessa was *his* by rights. Her willingness to be his bride was owed him. How could she turn her back on him as though his offer was hardly worth the breath it took her to refuse?

Lord, I pushed aside my own desires to shoulder my responsibility to Nessa and our families. I longed to choose my own wife, lay the path I'd follow, but knew it wasn't my place to flout the plan You had for me. I bowed to what I believed to be Your will. How could I make such a mistake? How can it be that my denying the desires of my heart in obedience to You have been an error? What did I misinterpret? Why am I struck so deeply by Nessa's rejection, when I scarcely wanted her acceptance at all? What went wrong?

Isaac slowed, turning the matter over in his mind. He breathed deeply, shaking his head to clear it. *What went wrong?* The points he'd made ticked through his mind, each as sound as the last until their combined weight should have felled any opposition. Had he not given in to expectation? What more could he offer than his home, his name, and his children?

Had Nessa, like an infant demanding some shiny bauble, tired of the prize as soon as it was within reach? Could a woman be so contrary? It wasn't like the girl he knew—always smiling, laughing even when she shouldn't, thinking of others, trying new things. That adventuresome Nessa wouldn't shy away from anything.

Isaac snorted. Even now Nessa hadn't shied away—she'd run. And how, exactly, was he to explain that to Pa? *I'm sorry, but the proposal was. . .*

ఇ

"Unforgivable, that's what it was!" Nessa's chest heaved as she drew Julia outside. "You'll never in a hundred years guess what Isaac Freimont's done now." She swiped at the tears trickling down her cheeks, angry at the sign of her own weakness.

"Don't tell me he made fun of your haircut!" Julia's horrified gasp brought Nessa up short.

Was it only scant hours ago that her troubles were so small? "No. He liked that." She waved the issue of her hairstyle away with an agitated flourish. "It's even worse!" She dropped down to the hay-strewn floor and drew her knees to her chest.

"Even worse?" Her friend's hushed tones spoke of a woman who now understood how dire the situation must be. "What?"

"The lout... Unthinkable—" Nessa blew her nose into her hanky and tried to form a coherent explanation. "Brute. He talked...duty, and—and w–work." The last word ended in a wail.

"I'm not following, dear." Julia gracefully sank next to her, offering a clean handkerchief. "What is it Isaac has done?"

"Oh, Julia." Closing her eyes, Nessa took a steadying breath before blurting out the terrible truth. "He proposed!" A fresh flood of tears welled before she could say another word.

"You wanted him to propose." Julia's reminder prodded Nessa's heart. "So why are you so upset now?"

"He doesn't love me." The grim revelation dried her tears.

"Surely you're mistaken!" Her friend put a consoling arm about her shoulders. "If Isaac's proposed, it means he *wants* to marry you, after all. This should be a celebration!"

"No." Nessa wrenched from her friend's awkward hug. "Listen to me, Julia. He spoke of duty and responsibility, expectation of the town, obligation to our families. Not a tender word of love in the whole bunch. Do you see?"

"He probably thought you knew that part already," Julia soothed. "Men don't often speak of such things. The fact he proposed must have seemed to him a declaration of his feelings."

"Perhaps." Nessa glowered. "Perhaps I could believe that if he hadn't gone on to speak of how it was a good time for a wedding, between planting and harvesting. If he hadn't said we could no longer delay or avoid the *inevitable*..."

"Ooh." Julia's quick intake of air gave Nessa a savage satisfaction. "That was an unfortunate phrase, but Isaac's never been the poetic sort, you know. He must have meant...

um. . .anticipated. Yes, he must have meant he didn't want to wait any longer before claiming you as his own."

"It gets worse," Nessa interrupted. "Isaac explained that we knew we'd get on well enough, since we've been friends for so long, and that we both knew what the true foundation for marriage was."

"Love." Her friend's voice rang with certainty.

"According to Isaac"—Nessa paused for dramatic emphasis—"the basis for marriage is a partnership to undertake hard work."

"No!"

"Yes!"

"No wonder you're all to pieces!" Julia blinked, astonishment painting her features. "Of all the things to say!"

"And even so, since I'd prayed so long and God granted me my greatest desire, I almost accepted him."

"You did not," Julia groaned. "Tell me you didn't!"

"I didn't." Nessa rose to her feet. "He saw my tears, you understand, and he told me not to be emotional."

"He must have been struck in the head." Julia hurried after her. "Isaac's wits have gone a-begging, for sure."

"Of course he's out of his mind," Nessa agreed. Tears pooled at her collar as she choked out her final word on the subject. "He couldn't possibly be his normal self if, after so many years, he asked me to marry him."

❧

Isaac snuck a glance at Nessa where she sat in a pew across the aisle. She sat straight and tall, her fancy hairstyle wisping around her face like a burnished halo. She nodded to friends, but Isaac saw the telltale signs that all wasn't well.

A tightness at the corners of her mouth reined in her usually generous smile. Dark circles smudged beneath Nessa's brown eyes, showing her strain. Most telling of all, she hadn't so much as glanced at him a single time all morning. Clearly, the disastrous episode two days before plagued her spirits much the same way it did his own.

Good. She should suffer in equal measure for her senseless actions. He'd gone to the Gailbraith home, the blacksmith shop, and even Nessa's favorite shady nook by the stream—all to no avail. How was he to straighten things out if she continued to avoid him? This would end today if Isaac had anything to say about it.

After church everyone exited the same doors. Isaac planned to hasten to the back and wait for Nessa to pass through. Then he'd snag her elbow and lead her around the building. With everyone about, she wouldn't make a scene of refusing to speak to him.

As far as Isaac knew, Nessa had been as close-mouthed about the whole thing as he had been. He tilted his head to the side, stretching his neck, and caught Julia Mathers glaring at him. *All right. Nessa told Julia. Women can't help themselves when it comes to talking.* At least he was still reasonably sure she hadn't told her family. *They* were perfectly pleasant.

"Good people of Saddleback," Rev. Matthews intoned, calling the congregation to attention, "let us raise our voices in praise to the Lord. Alma?"

Alma took her place on the piano bench and began to play a familiar hymn.

" 'God moves in a mysterious way, His wonders to perform.' " Isaac raised his voice with the rest of the congregation. *Mysterious seems about right.*

" 'He plants His footsteps in the sea, and rides upon the storm.' " The words mimicked the turbulence Isaac felt. Was Nessa's strange behavior a squall to be waited out? If so, what would be left of their friendship by the end of it all?

Isaac pondered the whirl of questions made all the more urgent by the words of praise. When the music ended, he'd found no answers. He listened as Alma began the next hymn.

All the way my Savior leads me;
What have I to ask beside?
Can I doubt His tender mercy,
Who through life has been my Guide?

Lord, it's not that I doubt Your wisdom. I question my understanding of Your will and Nessa's reaction to my proposal. Aside from Your leadership, I would seek understanding. Isaac prayed as the music swelled around him, coming to its close: " 'This my song through endless ages: Jesus led me all the way.' "

And He will lead me through what is to come. Some of the restless energy eased from Isaac's shoulders as he took his seat in the family pew.

"Thank you, Alma." Rev. Matthews inclined his head in recognition before he began the sermon. "Our praise this morning focused around man's inability to fathom the perfection of God's plans for us. This is widely acknowledged among believers. It is the next part that becomes difficult."

Without understanding, what can follow?

"It is trusting God's plans, following His path obediently, that is the downfall of many men." The reverend's words hit Isaac with almost palpable force. "When we do not understand why, it becomes a struggle. But it is not for us to know the ways of the Lord. We don't need to, for He knows our hearts. First Chronicles 28:9 says, 'For the Lord searcheth all hearts, and understandeth all the imaginations of the thoughts.' Our Father knows our needs and understands our desires, and He has plans for each one of us. We need no further reassurance than this."

All along I've prayed for Your guidance but not Your will. Show me Your path, Lord. Let this conversation with Nessa today make clear Your purpose, whether it be that we wed or not.

Swept away in the power of the morning's message, Isaac was surprised to see people rising from their seats. As politely as possible, he shouldered his way up the aisle until he reached the double mahogany doors of the church. There he waited for Nessa.

"Isaac!" Julia stopped in front of him and put her hand on his arm, trying to guide him outside. "Can you spare a moment? There's something we need to discuss."

"Right now?" He tried to keep his displeasure out of his expression. There was really no polite way to refuse a lady, but he had to catch Nessa before she slipped away. "I was hoping to speak with Nessa." He watched his quarry make her way toward the door.

"Ah," Julia sidestepped to block his view. Considering her impressive height and wide bonnet, she managed quite well. "To tell you the truth, Isaac," she said leaning in, all trace of good humor having fled from her voice, "I don't think that's a good idea."

"You're a good friend to Nessa." Isaac placed his hands on Julia's shoulders to keep her in place as he moved to the side. *Where is she?* "I appreciate that. But this is a private matter."

"All the more reason"—she spoke through gritted teeth, though her polite smile didn't waver—"*not* to force the issue in front of the entire community after church."

"She's been eluding me all week." Isaac pasted a smile on his own lips. "I've no choice."

"Of course you do." Julia pinned him with a glare. "And so

does Nessa. I suggest you remember that, Isaac Freimont."
With that, she swept down the steps.

Isaac scanned the crowd for any sign of Nessa but found
none. A muscle at the side of his jaw began to work furiously
as he was forced to admit that Julia's ploy had worked—Nessa
was gone.

four

All her life Nessa had seen the Freimont household as an extension of her own family. She loved the large home, brightened by plentiful windows, kept clean and welcoming by Isaac's mother. Delana Freimont stood as godmother and adopted aunt to her, and typically there was nothing Nessa loved better than to visit her.

Today she'd give her eyeteeth to be anywhere else. Nessa closed her eyes and drew a deep breath, capturing her doubts along with the yeasty warmth of fresh-baked bread. It would be all right—the women would prepare a midday feast and work in a quilting circle while the men went hunting.

After a long winter and late spring, there was not much left in their smokehouse. The men wisely put off hunting until after most animals bore young, so the thought of readily available fresh meat was almost tantalizing enough to make Nessa push aside her worries that Isaac had told his mother about his failed proposal. If she had to answer to Delana, so be it. *But it would be wonderful if it wasn't in front of all the women I hold dear.* Nessa cast a glance at her family as they approached the door. Rosalind Gailbraith and Kaitlin MacLean were strong, brave women Nessa wanted to emulate. Unfortunately, her mother and grandmother were also shrewdly discerning, and she'd been dodging their gentle questions for a week now.

"Come in, come in!" Delana ushered them all inside.

Amid a flurry of greetings, Nessa placed her basket of bread on a table already laden with baked goods. Aside from her own family and Michael Hornton's mother, all the women bore direct relation to the Freimonts.

Isaac's older brother, Brent, had a soft-spoken wife named Diane. His older sister, Marlene, was Julia's mother and Ma's best friend. Their surname was Mathers, but that was through marriage. As far as everyone in Saddleback was concerned, they were part of the Freimont family. It struck Nessa as astounding how young Isaac was when compared to the rest of his family. A seventeen-year gap between Marlene and Isaac made him the youngest by a long stretch. In fact, his nephews and nieces were closer to him in age.

"Nessa?" Julia's hug captured her attention. "I wasn't sure you'd come!"

"Of course I came. It's Saddleback tradition, after all. Besides," she lowered her voice, "I couldn't come up with an honest excuse not to come. At least, none Ma would accept."

"It'll be all right." Julia linked arms with Nessa, gesturing to the window. "The men are already gathered and ready to go, the younger girls are watching the children in the yard, and we'll be left to our own devices as soon as we've cooked enough food to feed everybody thrice over."

"Seems to me," Nessa judged, casting an eye over the tables loaded with biscuits, johnnycake, fresh bread, cinnamon rolls, and pies, "there's not much more cooking to be done."

"And Grandmam has rabbit stew already bubbling away." Julia surveyed the spread with approval. "Mrs. Hornton brought two of her own baked chickens, and Pa got down our last ham. Uncle Brent and Diane showed up with a wheel of their cheese, too. Looks like we'll be able to quilt and chat all morning!"

"Yes." Out of the corner of her eye, Nessa saw Ma and

Delana and Mrs. Mathers whispering together in the corner, heads bent. "That's what I was afraid of."

❧

"Brent, Johnny, would you go ahead and check the rabbit snares?" Dad took the lead, as he had since he founded Saddleback. "Ewan, Michael, Isaac, Robert, and I will head for the clearing and start watching for deer."

"Right." Johnny answered for himself and Brent as they shouldered their muskets and started off. The sooner the snares were emptied, the sooner they'd catch more rabbits.

Isaac gathered his things and set off toward the meadow. Keeping the hunting party small was, to his way of thinking, the wisest course. So long as only a small portion of Saddleback men came, there would be little noise to startle their prey. Even better, they'd not need to spend days trying to shoot and butcher enough for a dozen families.

Not to mention the fact that many newcomers, newly alighted from the railroad, still hadn't quite grasped the idea of selective hunting. More often than not, the greenhorns would shoot young bucks or mothers who would repopulate the area.

"You ever gonna tell me just what happened with Nessa?" Michael fell into stride beside Isaac.

"I already told you," Isaac said, glancing around to ensure none of the other men was close enough to overhear, "she said no. The rest isn't important—or at least not until I can talk to Nessa about what went wrong."

"That's what you said a week ago." Michael pointed out. "The fact that she's darted away from the sight of you presents an obstacle. Are you going to try to catch her today?"

"After the hunt, when everyone's finished working and full of good food. It'll attract less notice."

"Wasn't that the plan after church?"

"Julia interfered." Isaac's field of vision narrowed as he scowled. "She might stand between me and Nessa again."

"I'll take care of that." A change in his best friend's tone jolted Isaac from his own plans.

"Sounds like you've got something up your sleeve, Michael." He spoke lightly, testing the waters.

"I've had my eye on Julia Mathers for a bit," his friend admitted easily. "Always planned on asking to court her after you and Nessa were settled. Nothing like a wedding in the town to make a woman feel romantic, you know."

"Romance," Isaac scoffed. "You know her, she knows you—what do you need fancy words and flowers for? Just settle it."

"Hmm." Michael's noncommittal murmur didn't bother Isaac half as much as his friend's speculative look.

"What?"

"Nothing much." Michael shook his head. "But after that comment, I have an inkling why things went wrong with Nessa."

❧

"I must say," Grandmam declared as she ran a hand over the fabric before her, "that the wedding ring pattern is my favorite."

"Must be because you're such a romantic, Kaitlin," Delana chimed in. "And it's stood you in good stead—you shared so many happy years with Arthur before he passed on."

"Grandpap was a special man," Nessa agreed.

"Aye." Grandmam nodded. "And though I miss him still, I wouldna choose any different. 'Tis happy I am my own Rosalind found such a love in Ewan. Every mother wishes a happy marriage for her daughter."

Nessa closed her eyes at the talk of marriage, the hard lump of regret at Isaac's proposal choking her words. The women were circling around the topic of her and Isaac, preparing to draw out the truth. When she looked up, she knew it wasn't her imagination—Grandmam gave Ma a meaningful glance before Ma turned to her.

"Indeed." Ma never missed a stitch, even as she fixed her gaze on Nessa. "It is my fondest hope that our Nessa will have a happy home and loving family." She paused, and Nessa prayed she'd leave it at that. But Ma continued, "Your Da and I want grandchildren to dandle on our knees before too long."

An expectant silence fell over the sewing circle as every pair of eyes focused on Nessa. Not that she saw it happen, but she could feel the intensity as she focused on her quilting. The moment she looked up, she'd have to speak.

"With Brent and Marlene happily wed to their true loves," Delana ventured when the silence drew taut and uncomfortable for everyone, "I've grandchildren aplenty. All that's left to complete our family is a bride for Isaac." She heaved a deep sigh, which was followed by absolute stillness.

Without looking up, Nessa knew the others were not only staring at her, but they'd *stopped quilting*. Biting her lip, Nessa picked up the pace of her own stitches, plunging the needle in and out of the fabric with such intensity she couldn't possibly engage in conversation.

I am not going to give in, she promised herself. *I am going to sit here and sew until they start talking about something else, or*—She pulled her thread so taut, it snapped. In the stillness of the circle, Nessa fancied she actually heard a faint snap as it happened.

"That's all right." Marlene spoke from across the circle. "You're so far ahead of all of us it would do the circle good to have you stop for a minute. While you're rethreading your needle, we can chat about Isaac. It's hard to believe my little brother has grown into such a strong man. Mom's right—he's ready for a wife now. Don't you think so, Nessa?"

Nessa looked at the broken edges of her thread and knew she'd have to say something. She cleared her throat and made one last effort to avoid the conversation everyone else seemed determined to have.

"I know how you feel, Marlene." She looked up to find her suspicions confirmed. Not only were all the women staring at her, but they leaned forward to catch every word. "Why, Robbie has grown so fast I can scarce credit it. Thirteen already."

"Oh, yes." Julia pounced on Nessa's gambit. "Just the other day we were talking about how swiftly time passes. My own brother is growing by leaps and bounds. We're all so proud of him, aren't we?" She addressed the question to her own mother.

"Absolutely." Marlene didn't so much blink at the shift in topic. "All of the boys are growing so rapidly, but none more so than Isaac. I daresay Timothy and even Robbie look up to him as a role model. Am I right, Rosalind?"

"To an extent." Ma smiled at her best friend before fixing on Nessa once again. "But it is time Isaac set up his home and raised a family. Though we've not openly discussed the matter, I'd hope it won't be long before that happens. Is there any news you'd like to share with us, Nessa?"

She bit back a groan as she surveyed all the hopeful faces around her. There was no escape from answering the question. Nessa would have to tell them the truth.

"Well," she hedged, "I don't think Isaac will be marrying all that soon." Nessa pushed through the disappointed gasps to add, "At least, he won't be marrying me."

"Why ever not?" Grandmam abandoned all pretense of polite conversation. "Everyone knows the two of you are close, and something's changed in the past week. What happened?"

"He proposed," Nessa's words came in a whisper, "and I turned him down." She'd expected solemn silence to greet this announcement, a quiet even more oppressive and stifling than before she spoke. She'd been wrong.

"What?"

"No!"

"Surely not!"

All these exclamations, joined by squeals, shrieks, gasps, groans, snorts, and even a single inelegant "Huhn?" would have made Nessa smile at any other time. It wasn't often that someone stumped the women of Saddleback, Montana. Finally, the outburst calmed, leaving her Grandmam's soft question hovering between them.

"Why, dearie?" Those two words held a wealth of loving support and concern, bolstering Nessa so she could answer.

"I love him, Grandmam. I want to marry him." She saw the confusion in Ma's eyes. "But more than I want to marry him, I want him to love me."

"He cares deeply for you, Nessa," Delana assured her.

"As a friend, Delana." Her eyes filled with tears. "His proposal made it clear that he doesn't love me in the manner Dustin loves you, Da loves Ma, and Johnny loves Marlene."

"Surely you misunderstood," Marlene protested.

"No, she didn't." Julia said. "She told me precisely what Isaac said, and Nessa was right to refuse him."

"Such a thing is hard to mistake," Grandmam agreed.

"Love can grow in a marriage," Delana mused. "And you've your friendship as a solid foundation for that."

"No." Nessa rubbed her aching temples. "I want a husband

who loves me, not as a friend, but as a man loves a woman. Just as much, I want Isaac to have a wife he loves that much." Tears slipped down her cheeks. "I'm not that woman."

five

"*What* went wrong with Nessa?" Her brother's voice cracked, causing thirteen-year-old Robbie to flush a dull red.

"Quiet, Robbie!" Michael tried to nip the problem in the bud. "You know we keep our voices down when we're hunting."

"We're not at the clearing just yet," the youth stood firm.

"And time's wasting," Isaac agreed. "We'd better get going if we want to bag anything today."

"Wait!" Robbie stepped in front of him. "Nessa's been quiet all week, so I know something's wrong. Nessa's *never* quiet."

Isaac bit back a grin at the truth of that statement. "That's between your sister and me, Robbie."

"I should have known you'd said something mean." Robbie thrust out his chin. "The last time she acted so strange was when you laughed at her bonnet."

"That's different," Isaac protested. "I thought she was wearing that thing as a joke! Who puts a bird's nest on a hat?"

"Listen, I never said the hat wasn't ugly." Robbie crossed his arms over his chest. "What I want to know is what happened *this* time? What did you say to Nessa?"

"It's not so much what I said, as what she did." Isaac revealed as much as he intended to. This conversation was over.

"Oh?" Ewan Gailbraith put a hand on Robbie's shoulder. "And what did my daughter say, Isaac? I wouldn't intrude, but Nessa has been glum lately, and if she's been rude, it's my responsibility to see she rectifies her mistake."

She made a mistake, all right, Isaac reflected, *but you can't force her to become my fiancée.* Aloud, he said, "It's not a matter of manners, Mr. Gailbraith."

"It is if she insulted you, Isaac." Pa had obviously realized nobody followed him and doubled back. "You've been out of sorts yourself. If either of you has been rude to the other, it's past time you should have worked it out. We won't have this tension between our families. Did she offend you?"

I'd say she offended me—how much more insulting can a woman be than to tell a man she doesn't want to marry him?

"It's more a matter of pride," Michael explained.

"There's no room for pride in Saddleback," Pa said. "It puts distance between friends and strain between neighbors."

"Aye," Ewan agreed. "Proverbs says, 'A man's pride shall bring him low: but honour shall uphold the humble in spirit.'" He, Pa, and Robbie all looked at Isaac expectantly.

"I decided it was time Nessa and I got married, and she felt differently." He spit the words out in a rush.

"*That's* the problem?" Robbie hooted. "You're climbing the wrong fence there. Nessa does so want to marry you."

"That's what I thought, too." Isaac's jaw clenched. "We're both wrong. Now that everyone knows, we can leave it be and go hunting like we planned." *I know I feel like shooting something.*

"Wait a moment, lad." Ewan put out his paw of a hand. "You mean to say you proposed—proper—and Nessa turned you down?"

"I got down on one knee and everything," Isaac muttered.

"Then where did it go wrong?" Pa took off his hat to scratch his head. "Must be something I'm missing."

Isaac turned to Michael with raised brows.

"How should I know?" Michael shrugged. "You haven't told me anything more than that. I had wondered if you'd given her a proper proposal, is all, and you say you have."

"I did. Down on one knee, asked her to marry me... What more does a woman want than that? I mentioned children even!"

"What else did you say, exactly?" Ewan's brows knit together in concentration. "And what did Nessa say to you?"

"She mostly listened. Until she said she couldn't marry me and ran off." His hand closed into a fist.

"All right, then it must have been something you said." Michael sounded reasonable enough, but Isaac glowered at the implication that he'd botched his own proposal.

"I did everything right—held her hand, cupped her cheek, wiped her tears—"

"Tears?" Ewan's angry rumble interrupted him. "She cried? What did you say that made my little girl cry?"

"I spoke of joining our families, asked her to stand before the town as my wife." Isaac's fist knocked against a nearby tree with every point he made. "When she hesitated, I reminded her of our long-standing friendship and told her how certain I was that we could work alongside one another to build a life. What could possibly have been wrong with that?"

"Sounds good to me," Robbie put in. "And you said you mentioned kids, right? 'Cause Nessa wants lots of babies."

"Yes, I said that." Isaac rubbed his chin with his hand and noticed blood oozing from scrapes in his knuckles. "I thought she was crying because she was happy."

"She should have been happy," Pa agreed. "Sounds like a well-thought-out, sincere proposal. You took her wants and feelings into account and assured her you'd work hard for your family. What more could a girl want?"

æ

"More, please." Nessa drank deeply of the sun-warmed water, scarcely registering the tinny flavor as she handed the cup back to a young boy. "Thank you." Most of the water they'd drawn was boiling over one of the many fires they'd lit to keep flies at bay. Baskets of tansy and bitter herbs were scattered about for the same reason.

Everyone had eaten a light repast of bread and cheese as soon as the men returned, as no one wanted an over-full stomach for the work to come. The men had come back with a bighorn sheep and a sizable elk, both older males.

They bled both at the same time, putting the blood aside to make sausage later. Nessa and the other women tried to keep things as clean as possible, rinsing and hanging the hides as the men skinned both animals, taking the organs while they dressed the kills.

Nessa threw herself into the work, glad to have a task that occupied her hands and her mind. She took the length of elk intestine, flushing water through it time and time again until the water ran clear. Then she rinsed it a few more times just to be safe before she placed it in a bucket. She repeated the process with the sheep entrails while the other women cleaned the other organs.

A great deal of blood, dirt, water, and hard work later, the men finished butchering the meat and hanging it in the near-bursting smokehouse. Delana put the fragile livers in her icebox, declaring she'd make liverwurst the next day. Nessa bit back a grimace as she helped ready the feast for that evening. Everyone had brought a change of clothes, and the garments soiled with blood were already soaking in cold water to avoid stains.

When everyone was worn out and washed up, they sank

onto the benches with sighs of pleasure. Nessa couldn't tell which made the men happier—to be at rest or to have so much good food in front of them. Oh, who was she fooling? The meaty musk of smoked ham mingled with the pungent aromas of succulent roast chicken and rabbit stew layered over yeasty bread. The wholesome scent of creamy mashed potatoes begging to be drowned in thick, hearty gravy. Her mouth watered as Dustin Freimont blessed the meal.

"Dear Lord, we thank You for the bounty we're about to receive. We're glad to share it with our good neighbors and even better friends after a hard day's work. The success of our hunt belongs to You. Thank You for Your provision and love. Amen."

There was very little speaking for the next twenty minutes as all filled their plates and emptied them almost as rapidly. It wasn't until the women had cleared the table and brought out dessert that conversation and laughter joined the heady fragrances of cinnamon, buttery pastry, and strong coffee filling the air.

Still, Nessa didn't join in. She placed a forkful of apple pie in her mouth, savoring the sweet cinnamon and flaky crust, drawing out her enjoyment so she wouldn't have to speak. That wasn't nearly as difficult as pretending she didn't notice the concerned glances the women shot her way, and—more disheartening still—the puzzled expressions from the men.

Isaac, in sharp contrast to everyone else, didn't so much as look at her. Obviously, he'd told the men about her rejection. Still more apparent, he no longer wished to speak with her. Gone was the man who'd shadowed her footsteps for the past week, seeking to set things right. Something had changed with him. Perhaps he'd realized what she'd been mourning for days—he didn't really want to marry her. Maybe he wasn't looking at her because he wanted to spare her the gleam of relief in his eyes.

Nessa put down her fork, leaving half her pie untouched as she murmured an excuse and left the table. She walked toward the outhouse but veered off toward the far corner of the yard once she was out of sight. Wrapping her arms around her waist, she hunched against the cold of the night, the chill claiming her heart.

> *"Irish wishes are prayers indeed,*
> *And this especially true,*
> *When the wishes are made and sent*
> *On any day to You."*

Nessa recited the old rhyme her da had taught her, looking up to the sky as she spoke. "Lord, I'm speeding my prayers to You tonight. Before, when I asked You for my dearest wish—that Isaac and I would wed—I meant it in earnest. But now I see that my prayers were self-serving.

"All along I should have asked for the guidance to do Your will—not my own. Now Isaac has proposed, and the distance between us is growing greater than ever before. I blame my own childish wishing. If it is Your gracious plan that Isaac come to love me as I do him, I'll rejoice in it. But if that is not to be, Father, let my heart make room for the man of Your choosing."

The chill left her as she prayed, and she unwrapped her arms from about herself when she finished. Not quite ready to return to the others, she moved toward a whispering aspen. Fingering a fragile leaf, engrossed in the way it captured the silvery gild of moonlight, she didn't notice her father's approach until she heard his voice.

"Nessa?" He stood beside her. "Are you all right? Isaac mentioned his. . .er. . .the difficulty between you."

"I'd thought as much." She released the paper-thin leaf to pat her father's arm and strove to inject a lighthearted note in her voice. "Believe it or not, I've been the recipient of a great many odd glances this evening."

"Are we so transparent, then?" Da shook his head.

"To those who love you," Nessa answered. "The women cornered me in the sewing circle, you know."

"What a polite battle that must have been."

"Indeed. And all through dinner I sat silent, with hardly a word spoken to me after the great revelation of Isaac's proposal."

" 'Twasn't the proposal that stunned us, sweetheart." He placed an arm around her shoulders. "And none of us meant to make you feel awkward or left out."

"Oh no. Quite the contrary." Her first real grin of the day made her cheeks ache. "The men were trying to avoid the topic altogether, and the women were trying to refrain from smothering me with advice. I don't know which group had the more difficult challenge."

"I'd say the women were trying to keep their opinions to themselves," Da chuckled. "It won't last long, you know."

"Yes." Nessa sighed. "I fully expect to be cornered again in the near future. Probably when we get home. Ma's fit to burst at the seams, trying to hold it all in."

"Isn't it surprising that I got to you first?"

"Mmm," Nessa murmured noncommittally. "And what words of wisdom have you, the representative for the men of North Saddleback?" She softened the words with a smile. In all honesty, Nessa hoped her father was privy to knowledge beyond her understanding. Perhaps he could set everything to rights, the way he did whenever she was hurt as a child.

"So solemn you make it sound, and yet I take my position as your father more seriously than any friendship I hold dear. I cherish you, Vanessa Gilda Gailbraith." He gave her a squeeze before releasing her and shifting to face her. "And any man who wouldn't do the same doesn't deserve your hand."

She couldn't hold back her gasp. "How does Isaac know why I refused him?" She'd thought he'd never unravel her reasoning without someone to tug him into place.

"He doesn't." Da gave a deep sigh. "But when he related his proposal, there was only one thing missing as could make you deny the very man you've wanted so long."

"I don't know that there was only one thing wrong with it," Nessa frowned. "But that was the main problem, yes. Did you tell him?"

"No. Some things a man has to figure out for himself."

"What am I to do, Da?" She rested her head against his shoulder, just as she had when she was a little girl and he'd gathered her in his arms to chase away the hurt of a burnt finger or twisted ankle. "I can't bear to explain to him that he doesn't love me. It was already too hard admitting it to myself."

"You pray and you wait and you see how God will move Isaac's heart." Da put his hands on her shoulders and stepped back, forcing her to meet his gaze. "He may not realize the depth of his feelings for you, Nessa, but a man doesn't propose lightly. Your refusal will make him search his soul for the reason, and I think you were wise to tell him no. In time Isaac should come to see that he loves you."

"You think so?" She gulped back the tears that rose once more from the small part of herself that still hoped Isaac would come for her.

" 'Boast not thyself of to morrow; for thou knowest not what a day may bring forth,'" her father quoted. "Proverbs reminds us that we can't know what the future holds, but we can have faith in the Lord, who will see us through it."

six

"Mr. Hepplewhite." Isaac tipped his hat. Rumor had it that Saddleback's newest widower had tired of a life of luxury and wanted the adventure of the West. If that was so, the man would need good sense and better neighbors to make a go of it.

"Mr. Freimont," the older man acknowledged, a glint of amusement in his gray eyes. "I can see I was right in my initial estimation of the town population."

"Oh?" Pa raised a brow.

"If I forget a man's name, the best thing I can do is try Mr. Freimont."

"Hardly," Isaac grinned. "There are only three of us—Pa, Brent, and myself. Unless you're including my nephews." His brow furrowed at the thought, since two of his nephews were scarce years younger than himself.

"That's what I thought," Hepplewhite chortled. "One of the perks of founding the town, I'd say. Ah." He motioned to a well-dressed man about Isaac's age, and the fellow immediately headed toward them. "Here's the other Mr. Hepplewhite, my son, Lawrence." His father beamed with pride. "Lawrence, Misters Dustin and Isaac Freimont."

"Pleased to meet you." Lawrence shook hands with a solid grip and friendly smile. "We're grateful for all the help the community is pitching in, especially since Dad arrived while I was fetching my sister."

"He'd already commissioned the house," Pa pointed out.

"This barn raising is the first chance Saddleback has to really come together and welcome your family. We'll all get to know each other pretty well while the men swing hammers and the women make a meal you've never seen the likes of."

"Sounds good to me," Lawrence agreed. "It looks like the whole town has already showed up—more people than we expected."

"Since the railroad came through, Saddleback's been growing by leaps and bounds," Isaac pointed out. "And we're glad for the company."

"I'd introduce you to my daughter, but I'm not quite sure where she is." Mr. Hepplewhite scanned the crowd once again before shrugging.

"The women are probably flocked around her already," Pa reassured the man. "There will be time aplenty to socialize once the barn's built."

"Right."

"Hello, folks!" Mr. Hepplewhite climbed atop a pile of lumber to gather everyone's attention. "Now, I've heard that sometimes we perk up all this hard work with the spirit of competition. Sounds like a good motivator to me. What say the men split up into four groups of five or six. The first to raise a wall wins this bicycle!" He motioned toward a quilt-covered object.

Isaac blinked twice as a girl floated forward and pulled the covering away with a single, graceful flourish. He didn't spare so much as a glance for the bicycle; all of his attention was captured by the vision of loveliness beside it.

White-blond hair in perfect order, creamy skin kissed by roses, dainty features, and a full-skirted dress of pale yellow—Clementine Hepplewhite was the postcard for femininity. He'd never seen such fragile beauty in the hardworking world of

Montana, where men worked hard and their women matched them.

Clementine—and he knew that was her name, for he'd met everyone else and would never have forgotten such delicacy—was not built for work. No, such a girl would be protected, cossetted. She was the type of woman who needed a man to care for her. He stood straighter at the very thought, only tearing his gaze away when Michael stepped in his line of vision.

"Seems like you have one too many Freimonts," he joked. "With your dad, Brent and Johnny, and their sons, they've already topped six. What say you and I team up with the Gailbraiths and the Hepplewhites?"

"Absolutely." Here was a chance to show the Hepplewhites what he was made of, perhaps earn the father's approval and Clementine's admiration.

"I saw Nessa eying that bike," Michael continued. "Would be a nice gesture to win it for her—reestablish the friendship and so forth."

"Nessa wants it?" Isaac searched for her, finding her in her faded blue calico dress with her burnished locks escaping their pins with an ease born of practice.

Sure enough, she was keeping her gaze fixed on the bicycle. Isaac knew she would be stewing that she couldn't join her family's team to help win. Nessa had never been one just to sit back and let the men handle things.

"Yes, let's win it for Nessa," he said aloud to his team. *And for Clementine*, he added silently.

❧

"Don't look now"—Julia nudged Nessa—"but I think Isaac noticed your fascination with that contraption. He's joining your father and brother."

"Do you think Da may be right? That Isaac does care for me but doesn't realize it yet?" Nessa kept her voice low.

"I'd say it's a distinct possibility." Julia beamed. "They're taking their places now—Isaac, your father and Robbie, and the Hepplewhite men."

"And Michael Hornton," Nessa teased as her friend's gaze never left the one man whose name she hadn't spoken. "Surely you wouldn't want to leave him out."

"Of course not." Julia gave Nessa a warning glance. "Don't read too much into a simple oversight."

"Never." Nessa bit her lip. "Though I did notice your line of sight goes directly over to where Michael is standing. You must be struggling to decide which team to cheer on!"

"I've already made my choice," Julia murmured. Nessa's knowing look made her add hastily, "If it weren't for Isaac trying to get that bicycle for you, I would have rooted for my father and brother."

"Only proper," Nessa agreed. "But you've the soul of a romantic."

"Leave off and wave to Isaac in encouragement." Julia smiled toward Michael. "The whole team is looking this way."

Nessa grinned and waved, meeting Isaac's gaze before nodding at Michael, Da, Robbie, Mr. Hepplewhite, and his son. She felt her eyes widen in surprise as she found the stranger's gazed fixed on her, his hand raised to return her salute.

"What was Mr. Hepplewhite's name?" Nessa asked. "I didn't quite catch it."

"Malvern, I believe. Hard to forget, a name like that. Why do you want to know? You'll probably never need it." Julia squinted at the stocky, white-haired man as he gestured for the building to start. "Nice enough man, though."

"I meant his son," Nessa chuckled. "You know, the young, fairly handsome one working beside him? The man who waved back at us?"

"Ooh." Julia blushed. "I hardly even noticed him."

"That does it. You are going to stop pretending you aren't interested in Michael Hornton. If you don't even notice a handsome, eligible new man, you're practically smitten."

"Not smitten," she protested. "Just. . .interested."

"Finally!" Nessa elbowed her best friend. "I can't believe it took you so long to admit it, after all the years I've pined for Isaac. Well, at least now I can tell you I think he's noticed you, too."

"How's that?" Julia turned her full attention on Nessa. "What makes you think so?"

"There's a way he sneaks glances at you when he thinks nobody's watching. And he's mentioned several times how he wishes more women were of your height."

"Oh bother. If he wanted me, he'd say so. Not that he wants another woman who's as tall as I am." She demurred, but Nessa noticed how her friend instinctively smoothed her skirts.

"A compliment's a compliment. Besides, now you know he's noticed you. . .and liked what he saw." Nessa knew that if her friend wasn't wearing her bonnet, everyone would see that Julia's ears were turning bright red.

"Amazing how quickly they work, isn't it?"

"Mmhmm." Nessa was surprised to see just how much the men had accomplished while they'd been chatting. She tore her gaze from where Isaac and Mr. Hepplewhite—Jr.— were hammering nails into a support beam.

Both had removed their jackets, unbuttoned the top of their shirts, and rolled up their sleeves. She couldn't help but notice that Isaac was much broader and more muscular than the new arrival, his skin turned golden by his hours of work in the sunshine. Still, the young Mr. Hepplewhite had a kind of determined concentration she admired, especially since he was rather obviously unused to this type of work.

"We should go see what we can do to help out." Julia reminded Nessa that they shouldn't have been lingering in the shade to watch the men—even though the other three unmarried girls in Saddleback were doing the same thing.

"At the very least, we should introduce ourselves to Miss Hepplewhite." Nessa looked around for the girl, searching for her pale yellow dress. In all honesty, she'd been looking at the bicycle earlier and didn't have too much to go on.

"There she is."

Nessa followed Julia to a space farther back in the shade, to the right of where they'd been standing. She couldn't help but notice the new girl's porcelain prettiness. Nessa looked at her hairstyle and dress with appreciation. *Wonder how long she'll manage to keep that perfect coiffure and fancy dress from wilting in the heat. She'll probably manage far longer than I ever could.*

"Hello, Miss Hepplewhite." Nessa noticed she clasped a small hand gloved in white lace, of all things. "I'm Vanessa Gailbraith, and this is Julia Mathers. We're so pleased to welcome you to Saddleback."

"A pleasure to meet you." Miss Hepplewhite drew her hand back and nodded pleasantly to Julia. "It's good to see that there are a few young, unattached women other than myself. Why, when we stopped over in Virginia City, it was positively embarrassing the way men shouted proposals the moment they clapped eyes on me! So good to see this place is far more civilized."

"We like to think so." Nessa glanced at Julia for her reaction to this pronouncement. She gave a faint shrug and tried to keep the conversation. "It must be difficult to be the only woman of a household."

"Well, we do have Darla, but she's just the housekeeper." Miss Hepplewhite gave a small sigh. "It has been rather trying without another lady to converse with—so different from all my friends at finishing school."

"Such a lovely dress you're wearing." The ever-diplomatic Julia was quick to change to another topic so as not to defend the maligned Darla. "You must keep up on the latest fashions."

"But of course. I love to read *Godey's Lady's Book* and *McCall's Magazine*—that's how I learned about these gloves. Clever little things, aren't they? And so much cooler than leather." Miss Hepplewhite warmed to her topic. "I had these boots made specifically to wear with them." She lifted her skirts a scant inch and poked out a creamy white leather half boot. "Some say having mother-of-pearl buttons are the height of extravagance, but it matches the gloves, you see."

"Indeed," Nessa acknowledged, for the girl had turned her wrist to show two small mother-of-pearl buttons fastening her gloves. "I've never seen the like." *And never thought to. Those lovely things will be ruined and useless in less than a fortnight!*

"I do wonder how you keep your skin so fashionably light when you don't wear a bonnet." Julia must have heard the disbelief in Nessa's tone, for she shot her a warning look.

"Normally I do, but I have the most cunning little parasol— came with the gloves, you see." She reached beside the tree shading her delicate features and produced the parasol with a flourish. "White lace over satin, and the handle is mother-of-pearl, too. I simply couldn't resist it!"

"It completes the ensemble perfectly," Nessa praised. She hoped her smile didn't show how hard she was struggling not to laugh. Miss Hepplewhite was pretty as a picture, a walking work of art. It wouldn't be long before she became more practical in her attire. At least the woman was friendly, and Nessa put down her thoughtless comments to nervous excitement over meeting the town.

"I almost hate to ask, since we've only just met, but I've really no other avenues to seek such information." Miss Hepplewhite hesitated for a brief moment before making her request. "Could either of you tell me if that handsome man is engaged? He's quite appealing, in a rugged sort of way."

Nessa's gaze followed the new woman's gesture, straight to. . .

seven

"Isaac!" Michael bellowed and gestured for his friend to drop the hammer, indicating that they'd finished erecting their wall before any other team had managed.

"Done!" Isaac gave the last nail one more solid whack, feeling the force of the blow travel pleasantly up his arm before he put down the hammer and raised his hands above his head. There was nothing like healthy competition and good, hard work to distract a man from women. On that thought, he started looking around for Nessa...and Miss Hepplewhite. Luckily enough, they stood together, heading right for him. Isaac straightened his shoulders as they approached, taking the moment to appreciate the contrast between the two women.

"Miss Clementine Hepplewhite, meet Mr. Isaac Freimont." Nessa's introduction came with an overly bright smile, her voice sounding forced as she spoke directly to him for the first time since the "incident."

"A pleasure," Isaac responded as he gave a slight bow. He would've tipped his hat, but he'd taken it off to cool down.

"Such a gentleman!" The gesture obviously pleased Miss Hepplewhite. "When I discovered dear Vanessa knew you, I simply had to come congratulate you. You worked so quickly." She finished this with a glance of admiration. "Obviously, Mr. Freimont, you're quite accustomed to manly labor. Your expertise made up for my father's and brother's lack of it."

"I wouldn't say that." *But it's nice to hear you say it.* "It takes

53

the efforts of the whole team." He tore his gaze away from Miss Hepplewhite to see a sour expression hastily erased from Nessa's face. Thinking she might have interpreted the new girl's compliment as a disparagement to her father and brother, Isaac added, "And the Gailbraiths and my friend Michael are old hands at this sort of thing."

"They're more used to working over iron than lumber," Nessa allowed. The barest glimmer of a smile let him know she appreciated his comment.

"Would that be your friend Michael with Miss Mathers?" Miss Hepplewhite reclaimed his attention as she glanced toward Julia.

"Yes. I'd be happy to introduce you." He watched carefully for her reaction. Could the new arrival have fixed her interest on his best friend? Isaac caught himself frowning at the thought.

"If you like." She gave a dainty shrug but placed the scratchy lace of her gloved palm on his forearm.

Isaac took a minute to note the frilly gloves, which were almost practical next to the ridiculous floof of an umbrella she held in her other hand. *They must be dressing like this in all the big cities. Pretty little furbelows, but won't hold up out here.* He shifted his gaze to find Nessa already leading the way over to Michael and Julia. Seemed as though she didn't care a twit if he escorted another woman around. His jaw clenched as he started forward, only to have to slow to a shuffle to accommodate Miss Hepplewhite's tiny steps.

"Congratulations on your win, Isaac!" Julia addressed him after the obligatory introductions were made. "I was just asking Michael what you planned to do with your new bicycle." She cast a pointed glance toward Nessa, who was studiously avoiding his gaze.

"Why, didn't they tell you?" Lawrence Hepplewhite strode to join their group. "Isaac, in particular, was quite intent about claiming victory. I understood his reasons—and agreed completely—when the other members of our team revealed a unanimous desire to give the prize to such a lovely young lady." Lawrence stared at Nessa until his sister offered a formal introduction.

Isaac's lip curled in distaste as Lawrence bowed low over Nessa's hand. If the upstart had taken the liberty of pressing a kiss on her soft skin, Isaac would have stepped forward. *How did I ever think he was a good fellow? I should have seen right through his fancy manners and known he'd cause trouble.*

"Me?" Nessa's hopeful query diverted Isaac's scowl from Lawrence.

"Of course." His expression softened at her delight. "I know you've always secretly wanted one."

"I had no business wasting wishes on a bicycle when Da bought that incredible automobile. The Model T is a marvel. There's no need for any other source of transportation!"

"Ah, but there is a need to earn one of your lovely smiles," the upstart oozed. "There can be no greater purpose than to bring a lady joy."

"Oh." Nessa blinked at the man's fulsome compliment, obviously at a loss. "I would say that the greatest purpose is to serve Christ by loving our fellow man."

"But some of us know that a gift can be an expression of such love." Lawrence Hepplewhite recovered swiftly and showed no sign of registering Isaac's glower.

"Indeed." Miss Hepplewhite exerted a slight pressure to gain Isaac's attention, as he hadn't realized her hand still lay on his arm. "Especially if the gift is pretty. Don't you agree, Mr. Freimont?" She raised and lowered her lashes in a becoming show of modesty.

"Beauty is welcome wherever she walks." He smiled at her even as he wondered what possessed him to speak like a popinjay.

"Oh, Mr. Freimont!" She peeked up at him through her lashes. "Who would believe that such a strong man could be so gallant?"

"Certainly not I." Nessa's mutter was probably not intended for anyone's ears, but Isaac caught the words.

Since when did Nessa care about pretty phrases? He wondered. *And why didn't I know about it?*

❧

He never paid attention to me. Nessa all but rolled her eyes as Clementine flirted with Isaac and—*Good grief!*—he flirted back.

"Bicycles are monstrous contraptions," Clementine declared. "I can't imagine why anyone would want to try and balance on a spindly seat and two thin wheels. It scarcely seems safe!"

"Challenges are invigorating." Nessa bit off the words as her rival pressed up against Isaac's side as though afraid of the very idea of bicycling. "Good for improving character."

"Besides, it looks like fun to me." Isaac's support brought a warm tingling to her fingertips, a sort of itch to get on that bicycle and show him that he should be noticing *her*.

"Riding a bicycle can be very entertaining," Lawrence Hepplewhite broke in. "Though I've tried it only a few times, what little expertise I boast is at your service, Miss Gailbraith." His gray eyes, alight with interest, darkened when he turned to his sister. "Don't let Clementine's misgivings dissuade you from enjoying new things."

"After the barn is finished, I'd appreciate whatever advice you could give me, Mr. Hepplewhite." Her stomach gave an odd flutter at his admiring gaze.

"Please, call me Lawrence." He stepped a little closer.

"That's hardly proper on such short acquaintance." Isaac's protest should have irked her, but he'd shaken off Clementine's hand as he stepped forward.

"We don't stand much on such formalities in Saddleback," she reminded him, trying to control her grin as Isaac gave Lawrence a measuring look. "Particularly as his father makes a second Mr. Hepplewhite. Why, that's the reason we all call you and Brent by your first names. Your pa is Mr. Freimont. Same case here."

"Not by a long shot, Nessa." Isaac all but growled her name. "We've known each other for years." His emphasis on the "we" did not go unnoticed. "That gives us the right to address each other as friends."

Clementine sidled up once more. "Oh, but it's so fun to make new friends. And with Lawrence and myself so new to town, it would certainly put me at ease to have you address me by my Christian name. . .Isaac." As Clementine gave him a melting glance, Nessa abruptly began to reconsider her position on allowing such forward behavior.

"Perhaps—" She started to retract her earlier insistence, only to be silenced by Isaac.

"Clementine," his voice lingered on her name, "makes a good argument. We all want you and your brother to feel at home."

"I'm glad that's settled," Nessa tried not to sound disgruntled as Isaac gave her a cocky grin. "Lawrence." A burst of satisfaction streaked through her as Isaac's grin faded and Lawrence's widened in pleasure.

"I trust this will be the beginning of a close"—Lawrence paused meaningfully—"friendship, Nessa."

"*Va*-nessa," Isaac snapped. "Her given name is Vanessa. Family and close friends use her pet name. You've yet to earn the privilege, Hepplewhite." His words didn't make Lawrence so much as shift his stance, much less back away, which raised the newcomer in Nessa's estimation.

"Most of the town calls me Nessa," she pointed out, an angry heat suffusing her face. "It is our hope that the Hepplewhites will become close friends, so I've no objection to Lawrence's use of it." She didn't even look at Isaac, determined to flout his possessive posturing. How dare he try to make decisions for her. . .while another woman hung on his arm, no less!

"I have no pet name," Clementine sniffed. "They're rather common, you know. What reason to corrupt a perfectly good name with a pithy diminutive?" She gave a small smile, "Though 'Nessa' does have a sort of rural charm. I can see why you like it." The slight emphasis on "you" had to have been inadvertent.

"I do like it," Nessa agreed, "but can see why you'd rather not attempt a moniker. 'Clemmy' doesn't have the dignity of 'Clementine.'" She watched as the girl's pale complexion grew mottled. *Lord, forgive me for not regretting that.*

"I don't usually let people call me 'Mike.'" Michael attempted to salvage the conversation with a rueful grimace. "Puts me in mind of a mischievous lad."

"Which you were, if memory serves." Julia's tongue-in-cheek comment took Nessa by surprise, as her best friend usually subscribed to the role of peacemaker. But here she was, gently teasing Michael in an attempt to elicit his attention.

"The truth is no reason for saying so, Julia!" Michael's fond grin brought forth an appreciative chuckle from everyone.

"Perhaps I've more mischief than you realized," she

countered, eyes sparkling with triumph.

"Sounds like I'll have to pay closer attention." Michael shifted toward her, and Julia gave a soft smile.

"The women of Saddleback deserve every consideration," Lawrence agreed, his gaze fixed on Nessa. "When Dad decided to move to Montana, I'd no idea we'd discover such lovely ladies. If I'd only known, I would have hastened our arrival."

"We're gratified your family is here now," Nessa murmured. Out of the corner of her eye, she saw Clementine give Isaac a coy look. *At least, I'm glad you and your father are.*

eight

"I don't like that Hepplewhite boy," Isaac announced as he shoved a wheelbarrow full of ash over to a bare patch. He, his pa, and his brother, Brent, were liming the soil that would lie fallow this year. Turning up the loamy earth and spreading ash, pulverized limestone, or shards of seashells made the fields far better able to sustain crops.

"He's two years older than you are." Brent swiped a shovelful and shook it out, spreading it thickly on the overturned soil. "Seems wrong for you to call him a boy."

"Years don't make a man." Isaac dropped the handles with an audible thud. "It's experience. And Hepplewhite hasn't done enough hard labor and man's work to qualify just yet. I have."

"God has a different purpose for each one of us, son." Pa grunted as he lifted his own full shovel, and Isaac was struck once again by how quickly his father had aged over the past five years. "Lawrence Hepplewhite has a fine education and was a respected accountant back in South Carolina. He may not have swung a hammer much, but he's a quick study. I doubt you'll find anyone to say he's not as much a man as you are."

"He's going to have to earn my respect." Isaac blinked as a piece of ash landed in his eye. "I, for one, am not going to take for granted that he's a good man, or a welcome one."

"Isaac Bartholomew Freimont." Pa stopped shoveling, his tone ominous. He never used Isaac's full name unless it preceded a stern lecture—at the very least. "There is no good reason not to welcome a Christian brother to our town. What can that boy have done to rile you so quickly? Seemed like you and Nessa were getting along with Lawrence and Clementine the other day."

"That's the problem, Pa." Brent had planted his shovel in the ground and was leaning on the handle to watch Isaac's dressing-down. "I'd guess Nessa and Lawrence got along a little too well for my brother's taste. Am I right, Isaac?"

"He's overfamiliar with her," Isaac defended. "Not even an hour after meeting her he was already calling her 'Nessa.'"

"No man should disrespect a lady by using her given name without her permission." Pa frowned. "I'll have a word with Ewan about Lawrence's behavior. It doesn't bode well."

"Hepplewhite wrangled permission," Isaac admitted.

"Then it's Nessa's choice," Brent reminded him. "And if she's happy, you don't have the right to challenge it."

I should. He didn't speak the words out loud. If Nessa hadn't rejected his proposal, she'd be his intended. Then he could keep Lawrence Hepplewhite from sniffing around her. Isaac jabbed his shovel into the wheelbarrow, hearing the dull scrape of metal on metal. They'd need more ash soon.

"I still don't know why she turned me down." He muttered the bitter words, hating the taste of them but recognizing that he needed to understand her reasoning if he was to change it. If he wanted to change it, at all.

"Did you talk to her about it?" Brent nabbed the last bit of ash. "I hate to see you make the same mistake I did."

"Mistake?" Isaac straightened up. "What mistake?"

"I wouldn't call it a real mistake—it's what made me free to marry Diane, after all." His brother's defensive tone told Isaac it was a story worth listening to—closely.

"She's a fine wife to you," Pa affirmed.

"Who did you lose before you met Diane?" Isaac slapped his hat against his knee, raising a flurry of ash motes.

"Rosalind MacLean," Brent grumbled. "Once Ewan came to town, she didn't spare so much as a glance for me."

"Nessa's *mother*?" He shook off the strangeness of that concept. After all, Brent was eighteen years his senior. But the very idea that his brother might have... *No*. Best not to consider that idea too closely. Isaac shuddered.

"She didn't even have two years on me, remember." Brent shrugged. "Like you and Nessa, I always assumed the two of us were going to be married. Our families were close, there weren't many young women, she was an attractive girl... Seemed like a foregone conclusion to me."

"Makes sense. I take it she didn't agree?"

"Not so much. She and our sister were best friends, and Rosalind didn't see me as a suitor. When the railroad came through, it brought a lot of men. Our brother-in-law, Johnny, for one. Ewan Gailbraith for another. Anyone with two eyes could see the way he looked at her, and I determined to set him straight."

My problem exactly. "What'd you do?"

"Tried to claim Rosalind at an apple bee." Brent inspected the toes of his boots rather than look Isaac in the eye. "Told her to sit next to me, where she belonged."

Isaac sucked in a quick breath as he imagined how Nessa would react to an order like that. He then coughed on the ashes he'd inhaled, making Brent thump his back before continuing.

"I can see you get the idea. She told me she didn't belong to anyone then spent the day with Ewan. That day stretched into a lifetime." Brent shook his head. "Now that I have Diane, it's easy to see God's hand in my foolishness. But if you can learn from my error, I don't see any reason why you shouldn't."

"Any advice on what would work?"

"Wouldn't presume to guess. Not even if you promised to manure this entire field alone." Brent grinned. "You should know by now that there's no predicting what a woman will do."

ॐ

Nessa brushed the last of the dirt from around the sharp edges of the glass, then carefully lifted and set it aside. Beneath, the early potatoes—planted on April 10 as *The Farmer's Almanac* advised—were frost-free and thriving. She tilted her watering can and heard the gentle lapping of water flowing over thirsty ground.

"How do they look?" Ma called from where she was thinning the tomatoes. A basketful of the red vegetables sat beside her.

"Very good," Nessa answered as she headed for the pump and refilled the watering can. It was best to have the soil around the potatoes as soft as possible so she could remove them easily and move the plants to richer soil. If all went well, they'd have a small crop of early potatoes by Independence Day. "I'll be over to help you with the watermelon before you know it, Julia!"

Today Julia and Marlene helped with the Gailbraith garden. Tomorrow Ma and Nessa would go to their place. It wasn't a necessary arrangement—if the women decided to tend their own gardens, it would work well enough—but sharing the work made the time go by more quickly.

Nessa gently tugged one of the plants from its wet cocoon, carrying it over to the southern slope where it would grow best. She planted it next to the others she'd already moved, humming while she worked. With no one close enough to notice, she pulled off her gloves and tucked them in her apron pocket, reveling in the moist earth she shaped and patted into place. She'd put them back on when she needed to put away the plate of glass or cart the wheelbarrow around.

After she finished transplanting the potatoes, Nessa looked at her hands. Small and a bit too tan, with long fingers tapering to nails cut short, her hands held no pretensions. No milky-white softness here. No jewels to prove her importance. Callouses—not overly thick—protected her palms. Dirt lined her nail beds, no matter that she'd washed at the pump. She'd need soap to fully remove it.

Nessa liked her hands, liked that they showed how hard she worked for the people and land she loved. All the same, she couldn't quell a surge of disappointment at the sight of her bare left ring finger. A wedding band may not be a flashy adornment, but what it symbolized was more valuable than any precious metal or stone.

A lump pressed against the back of her throat as she realized, once again, that she might have thrown away her only chance to be Isaac's wife. Da thought Isaac would come to realize he loved her, but that was before Clementine Hepplewhite arrived in town with her delicate white lace and fragile beauty.

"Ready to work with the sweet corn?" Julia walked up to her and gestured to the hills she'd packed around the watermelon. Every five feet or so stood a little heap of dirt to nourish the crisp, juicy fruit as it grew into a summertime treat. "I finished about the same time you were done with those potatoes."

"All right." Nessa fell into step as her friend passed the rows of poles lashed together and covered with peas and beans.

"After we're finished with those, we can weed around the lettuce," Julia suggested. At Nessa's silent nod, she added,

"Then we can pick up all the slugs and keep them as pets."

"What?" She halted. "Since when have you developed a fondness for squishy, sticky, oozing, slimy garden pests?"

"I haven't, but there was no other way I could make sure you were listening." Julia nudged her with an elbow. "Since when do you quietly agree to everything I say?"

"Since I stopped trusting myself to make sound decisions." Nessa sighed. "Especially since you never put a foot wrong."

"What are talking about?" Her best friend gaped at her from between stalks of sweet corn. "If I had half your courage, I'd speak my mind often enough to find a little trouble."

"And if I had half your sense," Nessa retorted, "I'd know when to shut my mouth and avoid it!"

"You're thinking of Isaac, aren't you?" She sobered. "However difficult it is to believe, you made the right decision when you refused him. Where there is no love, there can be no marriage. On that account we're both right."

"That's just it." Nessa closed her eyes against a sour taste in the back of her throat. "I love him. Maybe I could have loved enough for both of us. Maybe he would have come to love me back. Perhaps it would have been better to live half my dream and not refuse it out of greed for the other part."

"Oh yes. I see what you mean." Julia's blithe agreement made Nessa abandon her hunched posture. "That verse in Ecclesiastes does say, 'Live joyfully with the wife whom thou. . .' What was that last bit again? The wife whom thou *likest* a great deal? No. That wasn't it. Maybe it was the wife who lovest *thou*? Nope. That's not right, either. Help me out here, Nessa, with the exact phrasing of God's words. He tells a man that he should 'Live joyfully with. . .'" She trailed off expectantly.

"'. . .the wife whom thou lovest.'" Nessa finished the verse, torn between crying over the fact Isaac didn't love her and laughing at the way her friend had proven her point.

That pretty much sums up the extremes of life—tears and laughter. My time to cry is over, she decided. *No more pining over Isaac.*

nine

Oh yes, it was time. Isaac waved to Rosalind Gailbraith as he stalked silently to where Nessa and Julia worked, half hidden among the corn. This time she wouldn't escape him. This time he'd wrangle an answer and hear her reason for refusing his proposal.

Julia spotted him first, eyes widening as he edged into view. To his surprise, she didn't warn Nessa or move to block his approach. Instead, she gave him a searching glance, followed by a wary nod.

She must believe Nessa is prepared for this conversation, he realized. His shadow fell over Nessa, making her look over her shoulder.

As Nessa rose to her feet, Julia tilted her head in silent question. If Julia left, it would be the first time the two of them had been alone since he proposed. What she saw in Nessa's expression must have reassured her, because Julia gave a small smile before brushing past him. She looked back once, a warning glint in her eyes, before she left them to the rustle of the corn and the heavy silence between them.

"Isaac?" Nessa spoke more softly than he'd ever heard her, the question in her voice belying her usual confidence.

"Nessa." Now that he stood before her, all the words he planned flew from his mind. He'd never seen her look this way—not happy, teasing, hopeful, peaceful, excited, angry, or even sad. Something more complex flickered in the depths of her hazel eyes. With a flash of understanding, he recognized it

67

as vulnerability. *But how can I hurt her when she rejected me?*

"What is it?" She prompted gently after he still hadn't said a word beyond her name. "Is there something you need?"

"I need you to tell me why you refused me." He gave up trying to sound detached. "You. . .seemed to care for me."

"I still do." She spoke more steadily now, sounding like the strong woman he'd watched her become.

"But you don't want me for your husband." If realizations could land physical blows, he'd be flat on the ground.

"No!" She sounded surprised by the very thought. "I've always hoped. . ." She gestured toward him then herself.

"Then why don't we?" He caught her hand in his. "What's holding you back?"

"You honestly don't know, do you?" Nessa tugged her hand away, straightening her shoulders in resignation.

"Is it that I didn't officially seek your father's blessing before I proposed? You see, I thought I already had it. I thought everyone wanted us to wed."

"Everyone but you." Her whisper tickled his ears, a plaintive murmur that made no sense.

"What gave you that idea?" He shoved his hand through his hair. "I proposed, I've sought you out since you refused, and I'm asking you to accept me as your husband. What other way can I show you I want you as my wife? You're the one who's putting a stop to this marriage."

"In a way, that's true. But my hesitation isn't the root of our problem." She must have read his frustration as she continued. "If you wanted me for your bride, really and truly, would you have paid such attention to Clementine Hepplewhite?"

"That was after you turned me down!" A dull pounding sounded in his temples. "She was new to town, sought me out while you were getting cozy with Lawrence! It has nothing to do with what lies between us, Nessa."

"It has everything to do with what lies between us, Isaac." She swallowed visibly. "And if you can't see that, then there's not much hope for us."

"You're being nonsensical," he growled.

"No, Isaac," she choked out the words as she turned from him, "for the first time, I'm being the sensible one." With that, she left him standing in the garden alone with a slug oozing over the tip of his boot.

He kicked it away, striding away from the Gailbraith home. Moving away from Nessa and away from the unshakable notion that he'd missed something important.

❧

Nessa didn't look back to see if Isaac would follow. She knew he wouldn't. It had been enough of a blow to his pride that she'd refused to marry him then come as close as she could to telling him it was all his fault.

Which it is. She harrumphed as she kept placing one foot before the other. Ma would know she needed some time to herself after her conversation with Isaac. Julia would tell her, giving Nessa the freedom to sort through the muddle of her thoughts.

First things first. Once she'd gone a reasonable distance—to the wooden bridge over their stream—she snatched up a smooth stone and flung it into the sparkling water. The initial splash faded into a series of soft plops as droplets caught the sun and dropped back. The stream, still full from winter's snow, moved too quickly for there to be rings upsetting the surface.

Instead, she spotted an alarmed frog hopping for safety, a thirsty dragonfly abandoning its drink, and a hungry fish streaking after its thwarted dinner. Her emotions taking their toll on those around her once again, Nessa couldn't help but see her love for Isaac as close kin to that stone. Both upset the balance of daily life, brought no joy, and left a sinking feeling behind.

I will not cry. Not for Isaac, not again. She sniffed as she made the resolution, stepping over the bridge to keep walking. *Never mind that not only does he not love me; it doesn't even occur to him that he should!*

She dried her tears with angry swipes, unable to stop them from falling. She trudged onward.

Oh, Lord, I've made a mess of it. But why do I still have this love for Isaac if it is not shared? You know me down to the number of hairs on my head, and I won't pretend I am without various flaws of character. But You love me despite those faults. Am I so unappealing that a man—lacking perfection in his own right—can't do the same? Is there something I am supposed to do to win Isaac's love, or am I to transfer my feelings to another man? I pledged to follow Your will, Lord, but I'm more bewildered than ever about how.

Nessa realized she'd wandered all the way to her Da's smithy when the scent of smoke wafted past her. She hastened to the door then waited a moment to allow her eyes to adjust to the darkness of the smithy.

The forge in the center of the room burned bright and hot, the smoke pushed up the chimney by rigged bellows. The thick stones encircling its heat held a clatter of tools readily at hand. Da, a bandana over his face, heavy leather apron and gloves catching sparks, beat a piece of red-hot iron over his anvil.

Robbie poured fresh water into the tempering bath, spotting her before their father did.

"Nessa! Did you bring us tarts?" He rushed forward, clearly

hoping for one of the sweet treats his sister sometimes surprised them with. When he moved closer, the smile dropped from his face. "You've been crying."

Belatedly, Nessa realized that some of the smithy's ash would have clung to the tracks of her tears. She pulled a handkerchief from her sleeve and scrubbed her cheeks.

"Robbie!" Da roared over the noise of the forge. "Come finish this for me!" When his son clearly had control over the piece, he pulled down his bandana and took Nessa's elbow.

The bandana was unique to her father and Robbie, made by Nessa's mother. Made of leather, save a small portion over the nose and mouth that was filled with regular fabric, Rosalind Gailbraith insisted the bandana be worn at the smithy. She feared that the weakness of the lungs that had claimed both her father and brother would seize hold of her family now. Nessa understood the precaution, as more than a few moments of breathing the thick air of the smithy set her throat to scratching.

"So he still hasn't reasoned it out, eh?" Da led her to a bench outside.

"No." Nessa offered a small smile. "You were right, Da. I wanted to tell him what the problem was, but he needs to know it from his heart."

"Aye. Is he any closer to understanding your side of things?"

"Hard to say." She twisted her handkerchief in her lap. "He wants to understand, made it clear that he wants to marry me, and believes that should be the end of the matter. Isaac's only question was why, if I cared for him, did I refuse his proposal?"

"And what did you tell him, Nessa?" Her father pulled off his great leather gloves and draped them over his knee.

"That if he couldn't see the answer, there was little hope for us."

"I don't suppose he took that too kindly, did he?" Da heaved a sigh. "But remember, Nessa, mighty works aren't accomplished by hope."

"If Isaac loving me constitutes a mighty work, things are even worse than I thought," she muttered.

"Ach, Nessa. Loving you is no hardship." He put an arm about her in reassurance. "Isaac knows he's blessed to have you in his life. The mighty work is where God makes Isaac into the husband you deserve."

ten

"The new tire arrived," Lawrence Hepplewhite told Isaac after church service two weeks later. "Mr. Gailbraith invited us over for Sunday dinner, so we'll bring it by then. He said you and Michael are welcome to join us. A little late to celebrate our victory, but better now than never."

"Unfortunate that you rolled over a nail when you tried to ride it over to Nessa's." Isaac bit back a grin at the memory.

"I like to think I recovered well," Lawrence defended. "Most men would have ended up with their backsides meeting the earth. You'll see when you have a crack at it this afternoon."

"So I will." He eyed the fellow with grudging respect. Lawrence Hepplewhite wasn't one to stand on false pride. Pa had been right, too, about how the new man was a quick study.

"There was something I wanted to discuss with you." Lawrence steered the conversation toward his real purpose. "Man to man, as it were. Can you spare a moment?"

"Certainly."

"Excellent." The other man rolled his shoulders as though to ease tension. "You seem close to everyone in the town, but I wondered at your relationship with Miss Gailbraith. Is there an...understanding between you?"

"I'd say there's anything but understanding," Isaac muttered. "Though—"

"Good to hear." Lawrence couldn't contain his satisfaction. "The way you and Clementine get along, I had hoped Nessa

73

was free to receive other attention. Didn't want to step on your toes, you know. Wouldn't be honorable to interfere if there was already an arrangement made there."

"Right." Isaac gritted his teeth. "To tell the truth—" He didn't get out another word before Lawrence steamed ahead.

"Not that I'm going to question my good fortune, but it seems odd. For the life of me, I can't comprehend why such a fine woman hasn't been snapped up already."

"It hasn't been for lack of trying," he divulged.

"Well, faint heart ne'er won fair maiden, and all that." Hepplewhite straightened his hat brim. "Something you might want to remember yourself, Freimont."

"What are you implying?" His comment stopped Isaac from clarifying that he still might be interested in courting Nessa. For the man to hint that Isaac hadn't been brave enough to pursue what he wanted was ludicrous. It hadn't been lack of courage on Isaac's part that caused Nessa to balk. That much was certain.

"Wasn't implying anything in particular." Hepplewhite grinned. "Just so happens I know Clementine will be very pleased to hear you'll be joining us for dinner."

"A lovely woman, your sister," Isaac praised. "It will be a pleasure to share her company this afternoon."

"I'll mention you said so. Until then."

"Yes." Isaac watched the other man walk away, acutely aware that Hepplewhite had been unwilling to hear Isaac express interest in Nessa. *If she'd accepted my proposal, I wouldn't have to make a claim,* he fumed. *But since she didn't, I don't have the grounds to tell Lawrence to back off.*

Almost a month had passed since she'd rebuffed his proposal, and she still wouldn't explain her reasons. The way things stood, if Nessa returned the interest of Saddleback's newest bachelor, Isaac couldn't do much about it.

"Isaac," a feminine purr shook him from his thoughts. "I'm so glad to hear we'll be spending the afternoon together."

"Clementine,"—he tipped his hat in acknowledgment—"you're looking well today."

"Oh, this old thing?" She ran a gloved hand over pale purple satin skirts. "So kind of you to say so."

"I wouldn't say it if it weren't true." Isaac smiled at the look of consternation on her face. "It's one of the reasons I'm not known for my fancy compliments."

"Then shame on the women who've neglected to give you cause to use them, I'd say." She dimpled up at him.

"It wasn't my intention to give you the idea that our ladies aren't lovely in their own right." Isaac frowned.

"Of course they are!" Clementine patted his arm. "Why, take Nessa, for example. Her natural charm shines through despite her worn clothing and browned skin. Quite a departure from the fashion, I know, but Lawrence seems quite taken with her."

"Fashion doesn't concern Nessa overmuch," Isaac admitted. Her simple dress and uncomplicated hairstyle weren't as intricate or elegant as Clementine's. That was obvious at a glance. All the same, she looked as pretty as she ever had.

"Indeed," she replied as her brother spoke to Nessa. "Sometimes we all need to reevaluate our priorities."

"Clementine," Isaac said as Nessa laughed at something Lawrence said, leaning close to him, "I couldn't agree more."

❧

"Of course you can!" Nessa dished out a second helping of rhubarb pie, handing the plate to Lawrence.

"Thank you." He slid his fork into the creamy filling with a murmur of approval. "Haven't tasted anything this good since the barn raising. Darla has a way with roasts and stews and such, but pie...that's another matter entirely."

"I'd rather not have a house full of sweets," Clementine announced. "Besides, our housekeeper does the best she can. If she falls short of the mark from time to time, that's to be expected." She raised her cup to her lips for a small sip.

"It was my intent to praise our hostess, not disparage Darla." Lawrence set his fork down. "Nor should you."

"We all fall short of the mark now and again," Isaac interjected. "I'm certain that's all Clementine meant."

"Precisely," she nodded virtuously. "Though there's little enough to do around here, I wonder her cooking doesn't improve."

"We always find something to occupy us," Nessa puzzled. "And while you're setting up your home, I can scarcely imagine you don't find your hands full long into the evening."

"Oh, Darla takes care of all that." Clementine waved her hand dismissively. "It's what a housekeeper is for."

"Right." Mr. Hepplewhite nodded enthusiastically. "Exactly why I offered her a substantial raise to come to Montana with us. Good help is hard to find, and industrious as Darla is, she has mentioned that there are scarcely enough hours in a day."

"Perhaps if you are dissatisfied with her baking, as she works so hard on other projects, you could step in." Ma addressed the suggestion to Clementine, whose eyes widened.

"Why would I do her work for her?" She set her cup down.

"You've time to fill, and helping another person is always worthwhile." Grandmam fixed Clementine with a gimlet eye. "Besides, if you think Darla's cooking isn't good enough, why would you sit back and let your father and brother make do?"

"Because she can't cook." Lawrence's dry tone would have had Nessa chuckling if she weren't so taken aback.

"Surely you exaggerate, Lawrence." Isaac swiftly came to Clementine's defense.

"No, he doesn't." Mr. Hepplewhite clapped one hand to his well-fed stomach. "Clementine could charm the birds from the trees, but she wouldn't be able to make a meal of them."

By this point, the girl flushed rosy pink, with even Isaac taken aback by this unwelcome revelation.

Nessa couldn't help but feel responsible for having inadvertently caused this conversation. "We've all had our share of mishaps in the kitchen," she heard herself saying. "The next time you find yourself lacking a pastime, I'd be glad to give you some suggestions. Cooking is much more enjoyable when you've others around."

"Whenever you like," Grandmam seconded.

"You'll be able to whip up a home-cooked meal after a few sessions," Ma assured her, not noticing that Clementine's becoming blush bled from her face with each comment.

If the girl became any paler, Nessa feared she'd faint. For the first time, she wondered whether Clementine's impressive curves and teensy waist were enhanced by a corset. Most women had eschewed the rigid confines in favor of comfort, but it did seem that Miss Hepplewhite's preoccupation with appearance hid a surprise or two.

"Oh, I—I c–couldn't," she stammered.

"Of course you could." Isaac remained oblivious to his dinner partner's distress. "The Gailbraith's are great cooks, and they don't give invitations they don't mean."

"Unless you'd like to practice in your own home, with Darla," Nessa intervened. "The more comfortable you are, the better the results will be, I'm sure."

"Perhaps." Clementine's color began to return. "Once things settle down and Darla's not so busy, I'll ask her."

"Where is Darla this afternoon?" Nessa remembered seeing the thin woman with mouse-brown hair at church. "Enjoying her afternoon off, I suppose? Next time we'll have to be sure she knows she's welcome to join us."

"The housekeeper?" Clementine all but squeaked.

"Why not?" Da rumbled. "She sounds like a good, hardworking woman. You'll find we value those traits in Saddleback."

"My mother was housekeeper and cook to Delana's family years ago." Grandmam's chin jutted out. "And my father was groundskeeper. The Albrights treated us all like family, asked us to come to Montana with them. If they hadn't been such wonderful people, my Arthur would never have left me to come settle this place with Dustin Freimont."

"There's no reason why Darla should be left alone on a Sunday afternoon simply because she works hard for her living," Isaac added.

"No," said Lawrence, "there really isn't." He looked, Nessa decided, as though the thought hadn't crossed his mind and, more important, the realization bothered him.

He's far different from his sister. Nessa nodded. Lawrence was new to town, but she could see he had a kind heart and generous spirit. *Yes, Lawrence Hepplewhite has the makings of a fine man.*

eleven

Legs pumping, chin jutted forward as his coat billowed about him, Lawrence eagerly demonstrated how to ride the bicycle. He looked, Isaac decided, about as foolish as a man could. Riding a horse never made a fellow look so ungainly. He slid his glance to take in Nessa's reaction.

"Wonderful!" Her hazel eyes wide, specks of gold dancing in delight, she clasped her hands together in anticipation. Nessa's gaze never left Lawrence as he made a neat stop just before her and hopped off in a fluid motion. "You balance so easily!"

"Takes some practice," Lawrence admitted. "You have to learn to find your center so the whole thing doesn't topple when you lift your feet off the ground. I fell off the first time I attempted it." His self-effacing grin elicited a smile from Nessa.

Lawrence would have fallen off, Isaac speculated. A man who tried so hard to please others couldn't possibly be steady of his own accord. *Listen to the man trumpet his failure to gain sympathy. Didn't he know mistakes were to be learned from privately?*

"If you'd like to try, Isaac, I'll walk you through it." Lawrence issued the challenge airily enough, but Isaac wondered whether the other man had read the distaste in his expression.

To refuse would be churlish, particularly as Isaac wrestled with a stab of remorse over his unworthy attitude. He nodded with what little enthusiasm he could muster and straddled the bike. He kept his feet planted on the ground as he eased onto the narrow, but surprisingly well-padded seat and gripped the handles.

Isaac leaned to the left, then the right, experimenting with how best to keep the contraption upright. *Shouldn't be too difficult,* he decided.

"I find it best to lean forward a bit and sit further back on the seat." Lawrence's helpful advice made Isaac glower.

"I like to think I can manage just fine and remain upright." He stiffened his spine and placed one booted foot on a pedal. Immediately, the whole thing leaned, and he had to shift to compensate. "Then again, no sense ignoring good advice." He leaned forward slightly.

"Got a feel for it now?" Lawrence gestured. "When you're ready, push off with your support leg and then pedal before you lose momentum. If you slow too much, it'll topple over."

"Mmmhh," Isaac grunted as he shoved off, the bicycle suddenly seeming far too narrow and light to hold him. He plunked his foot on the other pedal and started to pump his legs as Lawrence had done. For a moment, the wind rushed past his face and through his hair, and it seemed almost as though he'd left the earth.

Thunk! He hit an embedded rock, the bicycle bouncing. Isaac steered the handles to compensate but miscalculated. With a ringing crash, he and the machine hit the earth.

He lay there, stunned momentarily, before the dust settled and he saw Nessa, Clementine, Michael, Julia, and Lawrence all rushing toward him. Isaac began disentangling his legs, lunging to his feet just before they reached him. He righted the bicycle instead of rubbing his bruised backside, making a show of inspecting it.

"Are you all right?" Nessa entwined her arm with his, trying to give him support. She looked him over. "Nothing sprained or broken?" The anxiety in her eyes went a long way toward soothing his battered pride.

"It'll take more than a tumble to put me out of commission." He couldn't help glancing at Lawrence as he spoke.

"Oh, I was so frightened for you!" Clementine took hold of his other arm, clinging to him with grasping fingers.

"No need, Clementine." He desperately hoped those weren't tears sparkling in her eyes. "All's well that ends well. I should have leaned forward like your brother suggested. No damage done save a knock to my hard head."

Nessa chuckled at the admission, but Clementine ran her small hand through his hair. "You hit your head?"

"Er. . ." He was so distracted by the soft pressure of her touch and the cool breeze touching his scalp as she lifted his hair, he found it hard to speak. "No, I meant it figuratively, that's all."

"Thank goodness you're unharmed!" She stopped stroking his hair, her hand coming to rest on his shoulder.

It was only then that Isaac realized Nessa had stepped away from him and now held the bicycle. Lawrence stood beside her, the two of them so wrapped up in each other they didn't notice the sudden silence.

All at once, Isaac's stomach lurched. Perhaps more had been damaged in the fall than he'd realized.

⌘

When Clementine had started threading her fingers through Isaac's hair, a muscle in Nessa's cheek had begun to twitch. So she'd let go of his arm, unclenched her jaw, and allowed Lawrence to draw her into conversation.

"Happens to most people their first times out," he was saying. "Unless you start slow, with someone walking beside you to steady things. I would have offered to spot Isaac, but he seemed the sort to stand on his own."

"So true," Nessa murmured. Isaac was the sort to stand—or fall—on his own terms. Until he realized he needed the loving support others offered, Nessa would have to watch him fall. "It seems your sister is doing a thorough job of looking after him now."

"Yes." Lawrence gave her a searching glance. "I wouldn't blame you if you decided to hold off."

Nessa realized how sharp she must have sounded. "Oh no!" Her fingers tightened on the handlebars and she moved to stand beside the bike rather than in front of it. "With your assistance, I'm sure it's perfectly safe."

"You've a healthy measure of pluck, Nessa." He grinned in approval. "It's rare a man is fortunate enough to behold such a melding of bravery and beauty. I'd be honored to guide you."

"You flatter me, Lawrence," she chided, her smile taking the sting from her admonishment. "But you do it so well, I can't complain overmuch."

"Flattery is a term for empty words." He placed his hand over hers, his expression earnest. "My compliment is sincere, Nessa." The warmth of his palm seeped through the thin stretch of her glove.

"Then I thank you." She watched with some regret as he removed his hand.

"If I may?" At her nod, he placed his arm around her, his hand bracing her waist. "Step over the center bar. It's difficult with skirts, so I'll brace you."

Awareness of his proximity thrilled through her. Isaac had never looked at her so intensely. Nessa dutifully raised one foot until she stood astride the bicycle. She looked questioningly at Lawrence.

"Now, take your seat, sitting as far back as you can while still reaching the pedals." He stepped behind her, bracing her waist with both hands as she stretched her feet toward the pedals.

Her breath hissed at the familiarity of the contact, absorbing the warmth of his nearness. Had he not supported her, she would have tipped over. Nessa hastily set her feet back on the ground.

"All right, Nessa?" Julia watched them with an odd look on her face, as though she, like Nessa, wasn't entirely certain it was a good idea to be so near Lawrence.

"Yes. It's a bit more difficult to balance than I thought it would be."

"I'll second that." Isaac reached out to grasp one of the handlebars. "There, I've got you steady if you'd like to slide off."

"She's doing splendidly," Lawrence objected. "I've things well in hand."

"I noticed." The dark look Isaac shot at Lawrence, who still hadn't removed his supportive clasp, sent a tingle through Nessa.

She tamped it down. Isaac didn't love her, had been absorbed in Clementine all day, and now tried to put a stop to her bicycle lesson? No. He could play dog in the manger with someone else.

"Thank you, Isaac," she brushed his hand off the bike as she spoke, "but thanks to Lawrence I feel quite secure."

"Then we'll proceed with the lesson," Julia seconded. "I'd like to see it step by step and then decide if I've the courage to attempt a ride."

"I'll brace you." Michael's hasty offer was accompanied by a narrow glance at Lawrence.

Nessa wondered whether her friend noticed. Either way,

Julia fairly glowed with happiness at Michael's words. Isaac could learn a few things from his best friend, Nessa decided.

"To get on with it, place your feet on the pedals again, leaning forward this time," Lawrence directed. "Concentrate on balancing, and when you feel you've got it right, I'll loosen my grip."

Nessa followed his instructions, wobbling from side to side but never falling with Lawrence supporting her. After a while, she felt steady enough to try it on her own. As Lawrence lifted his hands, Nessa wanted them back. Nevertheless, she gamely pushed off at a slow pace, pedaling immediately.

"That's it!" Lawrence jogged beside her, hands outstretched and ready should she falter.

Reassured, Nessa pedaled faster, tightening her grip on the handlebars and relying on her own sense of balance to keep her upright.

"There you go!" Lawrence fell behind, shouting instructions to slow down before she turned back and not to stop until she'd reached them once more.

The wind kissed her cheeks, cooling the hot rush of excitement as she skimmed over the road, instinctively leaning to one side or the other as she steered past the spring ruts. The sound of her heart thrummed in her ears, her breath caught at the glorious suspension of weight. It felt as though everything, all her worries, all her disappointments, dropped from her shoulders as she whizzed forward.

This, Nessa decided, *is freedom.*

twelve

This, Isaac fumed, *is a disaster.*

One week had passed since they'd ridden the bicycle, since Isaac had fallen in front of everyone and Lawrence had put his hands around Nessa's trim waist. The time hadn't done much to temper his frustration.

As Isaac stewed, Lawrence remained glued to Nessa's side at the church social. Worse still, Nessa encouraged the attention, her eyes sparkling, pert nose tilted to display those beguiling freckles of hers, and a smile on her lips. She'd never looked better, and it was all for Lawrence Hepplewhite.

"Isaac!" Clementine emerged from a crowd of admirers to place one small hand trustingly in the crook of his arm. "I've had the most delicious notion."

"And what would that be?" He patted her hand, drinking in the sight of her smile as she peeped up at him from beneath the brim of her bonnet.

"I've heard of this place called Columbia Gardens—do you know about it?"

"In Butte?" Isaac searched his memory. "Didn't the Copper King make a sort of amusement park out there?"

"Yes, but it's much more than that." She spoke more quickly in her excitement, "There's a fine hotel, a ballroom, even a swimming pool. Not to mention the carousel and roller coaster."

"I've always thought a roller coaster sounded like a great adventure." Isaac shared some of her enthusiasm. "Up, down, and around, whizzing through the air. . .thrilling."

"I could never bring myself to try such a thing." She gave a small shudder. "But it sounds as though there's something for everyone. I've spoken with Lawrence about making a trip there in the next week or so. We'd love to have you join us."

"I'd enjoy that." He rubbed the back of his neck. "The thing is. . .some of us were hoping to go to Yellowstone, now that it's open to private automobiles."

"Can't you do both?" She gave a tiny pout.

"I doubt I could leave the farm that long." He searched for Michael. "We haven't mentioned the trip to Yellowstone in a while. I'd have to check and see if everyone's still aboard. If I can't come to Butte with you"—he stooped to catch her gaze— "would you consider joining our Yellowstone expedition?"

"I'd so hoped we could spend some time together"—she caught her lower lip between pearly teeth—"without all the. . .distractions here in Saddleback."

Isaac noted her gaze flick to Nessa, who was now drinking some punch with Lawrence. *If Clementine comes to Yellowstone, there will be no way to exclude her brother.* "Ah, there's Michael. Let's see if we're still set on Yellowstone." He waved his friend over, noticing that Julia clasped Michael's arm.

"What's running through your mind, Isaac?" He sounded happy.

"Wondering whether we're still set to go to Yellowstone this July," he probed. "Nobody's mentioned it in a while."

"I was looking forward to it," Julia answered. "Nessa is, too."

"Then we can't disappoint." Michael patted her hand. "Next week would be perfect timing, too."

"Nessa's grandmother will come as chaperone." Julia waved to Nessa, who made her way toward their group immediately.

"Yes?" Nessa hurried forward, Lawrence stuck to her side like a shadow.

"We were thinking of making that trip to Yellowstone next week," Michael began. "Are you and your grandmother still interested in joining us?"

"Absolutely!" Nessa tugged on Lawrence's sleeve. "We've plenty of room if you'd like to see the sights with us."

"Clementine and I had considered Columbia Gardens." Lawrence glanced at his sister. "But I, for one, would rather enjoy the company of the Yellowstone expedition. What do you say, Clementine?"

"I won't be the lone naysayer," Clementine demurred. "Aside from Mrs. MacLean, will the six of us make up the entire group?"

"I should like to keep us down to the two touring cars," Isaac planned aloud. "No sense in making it a caravan."

"Small and simple," Michael agreed, his smile all for Julia. "Just close friends."

❧

"So tell me again what the arrangements are?" Grandmam asked as Nessa started to pack.

"Six days to tour the park, plus the traveling time there and back," Nessa reminded. "When we're in hotels, we can order our meals. On the road we'll have to fend for ourselves." She tucked oats, cornmeal, sugar, and flour into a large pot before replacing the lid. Packing space was limited, with seven people traveling in two cars.

Grandmam peered at what Nessa had already set aside. "You've got rashers of bacon, salt pork, and jerked beef in this sack. And this crate is full of eggs, I'd guess?" She gestured to the straw-packed wooden box.

"Yes, though I don't expect they'll hold up as well." Nessa frowned.

"We brought eggs in wagons," Grandmam chuckled. "If the

straw worked for that, it'll do fine now."

"I hope so. Julia's packing a crate of apples, two rounds of cheese, and some canned preserves and such."

"Sounds like you've got the food portion all figured out." Grandmam began filling her own trunk. "Best be sure you have your own things packed."

"Yes, I already started but was trying to decide what clothes I'll need," Nessa mused aloud as she considered her own traveling trunk.

"Don't forget a light cloak and a heavy one," Grandmam cautioned. "There're parts of Yellowstone as get right cold even in the midst of summer."

"Right." Nessa folded her winter cape and laid it atop her stockings, chemises, and petticoats. These were placed over a spare pair of half boots and her toiletry case. She tossed in an apron to conceal the worst of the dirt she'd gather on the trip.

"How much room do you have left?" Grandmam peered in Nessa's trunk. "Good. You can put two dresses in there and have three altogether."

"I was going to wear the blue calico and pack the green merino wool. That leaves the yellow cotton or the dusky rose dress."

"Take the rose," Grandmam instructed. "Looks lovely on you."

"And the yellow will show dust far more quickly." Nessa neatly folded the two chosen garments and smoothed them in. "Good thinking."

"I wasn't thinking of the dust, Nessa." Grandmam chuckled. "More along the lines of how that Clementine wears pale colors all the time."

"And I wouldn't want to set myself up for comparison to her ensembles," Nessa concluded with a grimace.

"Pastel is for girls," Grandmam corrected. "More vibrant

tones are for women. Darker hues hint at the depth of your character, Nessa. Besides, they look good with your hair and eyes."

"Thank you, Grandmam." Nessa kissed her wrinkled cheek. "Having you on the trip may well be my favorite part of it."

"I hope not!" She smiled. "Not with Isaac and Lawrence taking the lead."

"To tell the truth, I've been praying about that." Nessa added her travel diary and a sun hat to her trunk and closed it tightly. "Isaac has been the one I've loved since childhood, but despite my prayers, he's not shown the same for me. It took his proposal for me to realize I've been asking God for what I want, rather than seeking His will."

"So this trip will give you time to see if Lawrence is the man God plans to be your husband?" Grandmam peered over the top of her spectacles. "And let you see how serious things are between Isaac and Clementine, while you're at it?"

"Yes." Nessa gave her grandmam a hug. "Sometimes I wonder if there's anything in my head you don't already know."

"'Tis no special talent on my part." Kaitlin MacLean stroked her granddaughter's hair. "You've an open mind, clear soul, and honest heart. They speak for themselves."

"Even so, Isaac doesn't hear me. The longer he refuses to listen, the more I feel God nudging me in another direction."

"Don't be too hasty, dearie," Grandmam warned as she shut her own trunk. "Your grandda used to say, 'Slow and steady as you go, and you won't run into a gopher hole.'"

"I remember him saying that." Nessa focused on the memory. "Didn't he come up with that after you twisted your ankle?"

"Aye. Delana brought me to Arthur when she took herself

to Dustin. Added along with her younger brother, Mama Albright, and your great-grandparents, we were a sizable party. But when we arrived, we found surprised men, a single barn, dozens of gopher holes, and not much else."

"And you taking care of Ma, just newly born." Nessa shook her head. "Looking at Saddleback today, it's almost impossible to imagine."

"Time has a way of changing things." Grandmam sank into her rocker with a happy sigh.

Nessa thought of Isaac. "I hope so, Grandmam. I really do."

thirteen

"Everybody ready to go?" Isaac asked as they stood beside the freshly refueled cars. "We'll reach Mammoth Hot Springs before dark."

"Wonderful," Clementine cooed. "I can't wait to freshen up. I feel so. . .disheveled." She gave a moue of distaste.

"You look pretty as a picture," Isaac disagreed. He told the truth, as she'd smoothed her hair and shaken the wrinkles from her cream linen dress. She'd donned her bonnet before stepping foot outside the closed automobile, her skin milky white.

"It's so exciting!" Nessa's grin stretched from ear to ear. A breeze teased the soft tendrils of her hair, lifting them into a sort of blurry frame about her face. Her simple blue calico dress looked distinctly rumpled, and her hat hung askew from the ribbon about her neck. The sun had lingered on her face, leaving its ruddy kiss on the tip of her nose and the apples of her cheeks. Much more, and she'd burn.

"Nessa, it seems you've caught some sun." He cast a glance at Lawrence's open-air Model T. "Perhaps you'd like to ride in my closed-top for the rest of the day?"

"No, thank you." Nessa remarked coolly. "I like riding alongside Lawrence, with the wind in our hair and the road before us."

"We've had a good time of it," Lawrence agreed. "A man can't ask for more than enjoying a drive with two lovely ladies." His smile included Mrs. MacLean, who smiled back.

"And we've plenty of those to go around." Isaac looked down at Clementine. For the first time, he realized how short she was. The tip of her hat all but brushed his nose.

"We should get on our way." Julia got him back on track. She and Michael climbed into the back of Isaac's car, where they'd ridden for the entire trip.

Isaac gave Clementine an arm up, noticing Lawrence do the same for Nessa and Mrs. MacLean. He moved to the front of the automobile, grasped the lever, and began cranking it until he judged it long enough.

Isaac slid into the seat, turned the key, and listened with satisfaction as the car spluttered to life. *Whhhrrr, whhrrrr* gave way to a loud growl as it started, the force of the engine making the car vibrate. With a low rumble, the car was ready to go.

Isaac made sure Lawrence was prepared, released the brake lever, and then eased his Ford back onto the road. For a while, he lost himself in the pleasure of driving, the power and speed he controlled.

Clementine fanned herself, so Isaac reached forward and opened the windshield. The inch-thick panes of glass tilted outward, allowing a welcome rush of summer air.

They passed lodgepole pines, catching a glimpse of the occasional coyote, as they approached their destination. When they passed Fort Yellowstone on their left, Isaac knew the impressive structure ahead must be the Mammoth Hot Springs Hotel.

"I hear it's built right where the National Hotel used to be," Michael observed.

"Supposedly it's been remodeled entirely in the past few years," Clementine added. "I wonder what type of improvements they've made."

"Electricity and plumbing," Isaac speculated. "There've been quite a few advancements made." They drove past a houselike building with a sign proclaiming HAMILTON STORE and pulled up in front of the hotel.

"So many automobiles!" Clementine peeped through the window. "I'd have thought this would be more of an isolated retreat."

"I hear the number of visitors began to grow by leaps and bounds when they started allowing private cars." Isaac took his foot off the gas pedal, pressing down on the far right pedal to slow the car. The transmission slowed to a stop as they coasted into an open space. He set the brake before hopping out.

Lawrence pulled in beside them, giving a cheery *oouuugggaaa* on his horn.

After ensuring Clementine was safely on the ground—the car was high for such a tiny woman to climb down—Isaac beat Lawrence to Nessa's door. "We've made it." He clung to her hand until she pulled it away.

"Yes." Her smile broadened. "The start of a great adventure."

⁂

"There"—Nessa gestured to her small trunk and the one next to it—"those are mine and Grandmam's."

"Got them." Lawrence stacked one atop the other and hefted both, taking a step backward at the weight but recovering swiftly.

"This?" Isaac's disbelieving tone had Nessa turning around to see Clementine claiming what looked to be a massive steamer trunk.

I knew it! Nessa pursed her lips against a smile as Isaac unstrapped the monstrosity. *It had to be hers!*

"Yes." Clementine lowered her lashes. "I didn't realize the other ladies would be bringing so little."

"Good thing they did." Lawrence sounded muffled from behind the two pieces of luggage he carried. "Or we would have needed another Ford to carry it all."

"That's not fair, Larry!" Clementine's cry had the strange effect of Lawrence setting down the trunks with a thud.

Larry? Nessa wrinkled her nose.

"You know better than to call me that." Lawrence glowered at his sister. "Old nickname," he explained to the rest of them.

"We already established that we'd only use monikers if the person approved," Nessa reminded. "And so far, I'm the only one. Besides, it's obvious you've far outstripped your childhood name."

"Yes." Lawrence grabbed the trunks once again. "Let's get settled, then."

He led the way, with Isaac and Michael each grasping one end of Clementine's portmanteau. Julia's large valise slid around atop it alongside the smaller three satchels the men had packed.

"I don't understand why everyone is carrying on so," claimed a peevish Clementine. "They may not be bringing them inside, but I know the other women brought extra bags and crates." She kicked a pebble, sending it skittering in the dirt.

"They," Isaac grunted as he shifted his grip, "packed the food and supplies we'll need when we're not at a hotel."

"What?" Clementine stopped in the middle of the dusty walkway, forcing Isaac and Michael to halt or run into her. "I was led to believe we have accommodations arranged each night."

Lawrence emerged from the hotel, having set his burden inside. "We do. We've rented tents for the nights we won't be in a hotel."

"*Tents?*" Clementine pronounced the word in the tone

Nessa reserved for plague-ridden rats.

"Yes." Isaac mopped his brow with a bandana, having dropped the luggage when Clementine blocked the road.

"Girls in one, guys in another," Michael rolled his shoulders. "We'll be staying in hotels mostly."

"Such an exciting plan!" Nessa plucked one of the satchels to lighten the load.

"Let's get to it." Lawrence took it from her, every inch the gentleman. He grabbed Julia's valise, as well.

When he turned his back, Nessa snatched another satchel, with Julia grasping the other. Isaac gave them both appreciative grins before frowning at Clementine, who stood in the middle of the road, mouth agape, as though impersonating a statue.

"Once we get inside, we can rest and freshen up." Nessa's comment got through, and Clementine started moving again.

Everyone pretended not to hear Clementine's dark mutters as they entered the hotel. Within a quarter hour, they'd found their rooms and deposited their things. The men went out to hang their food supply in nearby trees to avoid attracting bears, leaving the women in their room.

"Satisfactory," Clementine pronounced as she sank onto one of the beds. "Though it's not a very large room, is it?"

"It doesn't need to be." Grandmam splashed her face with water from the washbasin. "And they said there's a real restroom down the hall, with full plumbing."

"Magnificent," Nessa breathed as she pulled the curtains aside and beheld the vista before her. A whole nation of pines stretched from the perimeter of the hotel to the hills beyond. Billows of steam puffed into the air from the one sparsely foliaged area. "Have a look!" She stepped aside so Julia could take in the panorama.

"Incredible!" Julia craned her neck to see the pillows of

steam rising. "Those must be the hot springs. And over there is the executive house. The president of the park lives there."

"I can see why." Grandmam replaced Julia at the window.

"Haven't you seen enough trees for one day?" Clementine peered at her fingernails. "That's practically all we've seen the entire day! Tomorrow we'll see some interesting sights."

"If you ask me, the mountains, pines, good earth, and endless sky are interesting sights." Nessa began to unbutton one of her shoes. "God's imagination is boundless." She slid it off then turned it upside down to see the source of her irritation bounce onto the floorboards.

"I suppose you'd think rocks are fascinating, too." Clementine watched Nessa pick up the pebble.

"To tell the truth"—she made a point of depositing the stone in the wastebasket—"I was thinking about how some of God's creations can be surprisingly irritating."

fourteen

"That's what she's called," Isaac insisted, addressing Clementine's question about the tall, peaked rock formation before them.

"Liberty Cap?" She scrunched her nose as she surveyed the rocky outgrowth before her. "I've never seen a hat that ugly. Who would wear such a thing?"

"The French." Lawrence studied the tall cone of the old hot spring. "During the Revolution, they wore peaked caps that looked something like this. Must be where the name came from."

"It looks almost as though a giant put his hand on it and smushed the whole thing down," Nessa observed. "But maybe it grew up in stages so it looks like there are different levels of it."

"That sounds like as good a guess as any." Isaac locked his tripod into place and mounted his Sereco view camera, adjusting the rack and pinion until he had the vantage he wanted. He tightened the milled-head screw and racked the bellows closer to the front for a wider angle, switching out the extra rapid portrait lens for the rapid rectilinear lens, which was better for landscape work. He checked his adjustments one last time before taking the picture. "Got it!" He carefully packed his equipment back into its carrying case.

"I hope it turns out well." Nessa tilted her head back for one last look at the towering stone.

"It will." Isaac snapped the case shut. "Miracle of technology— that's the wonder of photography. Quickest way to capture a memory and keep it perfectly forever."

"I don't know about that." Michael rested a hand on Julia's shoulder. "In the time it took you to set all that up, Julia sketched the Liberty Cap from two different angles."

"Fair enough," Isaac acknowledged. "What I should have said is that it's the best way for those of us without an innate talent for traditional art."

"Don't be so modest." Clementine linked her arm through his. "Just watching you set up all that complex equipment was more than impressive."

"Thank you." He soaked in her smile. "I also snapped a panoramic shot of the Devil's Thumb."

"That other great big rocky tower?" She peered as though it were far, far away. "I wonder why they call it the Devil's Thumb." She gave a little shiver.

"According to this printed guide, over thirty of the sites have names related to the devil." Mrs. MacLean read aloud. "Seems as though when they were discovered, the men thought them a good example of the type of fire and brimstone sinners might expect after death."

"I thought we were going to see pretty things"—Clementine nibbled her lower lip—"not what some people think is a representation of hell."

"No need to be afraid." Lawrence tucked Nessa by his side, and Isaac reflexively tightened his hold on Clementine.

"Not if your heart is right before the Lord," Kaitlin MacLean added.

They looked at the large formation thrusting up from the earth and unanimously agreed that it did resemble a thumb. Everyone relaxed a bit as they piled back into the cars and made their way to Mammoth Hot Springs.

That site, Isaac wasn't pleased to see, was far more crowded.

Getting a picture without people standing in the way or steam filming over his lens made him move back and be content with whatever came of it.

"Would you look at all the people who brought their bathing costumes." Nessa's eyes were wide as they watched people climb into the enormous hot springs, looking for all the world as though they were soaking in large tubs.

"It's supposed to be good for the health," Lawrence explained. "Would you like to try it?"

"No, thank you." Nessa's blush surprised Isaac. Apparently she didn't approve of the fashionable bath suits women wore, exposing their lower limbs to a daring degree.

"One of the hotels has geyser water pumped directly into real bathtubs." Isaac spoke up before he started to wonder how Nessa would look in one of those bath costumes. "So we'll have a chance to try it out later."

By the time they reached Camp Sheridan, a recently abandoned army headquarters that had been turned into lodgings for tourists, Isaac's stomach began to growl. He drove until he found a nice open space where they could set up a fire and make dinner.

"What's that?" Clementine squinted at what looked to be a cemetery.

Not for the first time, Isaac wondered whether Clementine's vision was poor. "The army's burial ground for the soldiers who guarded the park up until this past year."

Nessa, with Lawrence at her side, joined them.

"Why were there soldiers?" Clementine's eyes widened in fright, her hand grasping Isaac's sleeve. "Is this place so very dangerous?"

"No." Mrs. MacLean swept past them. "More like people are dangerous to this place. The army was here to guard the land, protect it against poachers and vandals. That type of thing. Started some twenty years ago, and they just left the post last year."

"So it's safe." Clementine leaned against Isaac in relief.

"Don't worry." He put his arm around her waist so she wouldn't sag all the way to the ground. "I've got you."

⁂

"Here you are." Clementine thrust a handful of bedraggled weeds toward Nessa. "Dandelions." Clumps of dirt fell from the roots, wispy seeds scattering in the wind.

"Thank you." Nessa took them and shook the rest of the dirt free. "It's a good start."

"Start?" Clementine ran a gloved hand across her forehead as though she'd been swinging a pickax all day. "How much more do you need?"

"We need about four quarts worth of the greens, rinsed." She laid them atop a flat area on a log bleached almost white by the sun and weather. "And it's best to pick the leaves of plants that haven't bloomed already. Otherwise, they tend to be bitter."

"How can you tell they're dandelions without the poufy ball on the end?"

"The leaves." Julia picked one from the torn stalks. "Low to the ground, light green, with lots of elongated round edges."

Clementine squinted before giving a hesitant nod. "Is there a basket or something I can use since we need a lot more?"

"Put them in the pockets of an apron." Nessa shook out her spare. "Use this if you like."

"All right." Clementine took the apron strings and wrapped them about her waist. "If you're certain this is all I can do to help."

"You can finish peeling the potatoes." Grandmam held one up.

"I'm not very good with sharp things." Clementine took one look at the brown lumpy vegetable and paring knife before wandering off. She didn't head toward the open areas where the most vegetation could be found.

No, Clementine made her way toward the cars, where the men were repositioning supplies, checking the tires, and making sure the engines didn't overheat. Nessa didn't quite know the whole of it, but it was obvious that they were engrossed in the automobiles.

"Valiant attempt to have her be useful," Julia commented. "She just snatched a handful of grass, though. Do you think she's foolish, lazy, or vain?"

"Given the option, I'd say she doesn't see this as important," Nessa said. "Though I'm not sure why you listed vanity among the options."

"Seems to me Clementine displays all the hallmarks of someone with poor vision." Julia rapidly plucked a patch of dandelion greens while she spoke. "All the same, she doesn't wear glasses. I wondered whether it was because she didn't consider them fashionable."

"Perhaps." Nessa recalled the way Clementine clung to Isaac's arm, giving prettily concerned glances whenever she surveyed things at a distance. *Can it be she's not acting frail but genuinely relies on others to navigate her way through life?* As Nessa filled her pockets with greens, she promised herself she would keep a closer eye on Clementine.

She busied herself with rinsing the dandelions, tearing the leaves before she added them to the boiling water. Clementine stood next to Isaac, as though she hadn't a care in the world.

"I'm ready to add the salt pork." Grandmam peered into the saucepan before dropping the small cuts of meat inside.

Nessa popped the cover over the entire mixture before

cutting the potatoes into manageable chunks. It'd be a while before Grandmam added them to the pan.

"I've set up the Dutch oven." Julia motioned to the cast iron contraption nestled in the ashes of the fire. "What say we use the milk we bought at Hamilton's this morning and bake some corn bread?"

"Sure." Grandmam began to pour cornmeal, flour, and salt into a bowl while Nessa went to fetch a few eggs.

"Nessa!" Lawrence straightened up as she approached, wiping his hands on a bandana. "I hope you've come to tell us dinner's ready. Smells good."

"I'm afraid I just came for a few eggs." She pushed aside the packing straw and carefully gathered a few. "The greens and pork need to simmer before we add the potatoes. It'll be about another hour or so."

"What're the eggs for?" Clementine fingered the leaves in her apron pocket.

"Corn bread." Nessa wasn't sure what to say to the other woman. *I've never met someone who abandons their work to others.*

"If I wasn't so sure you'd send me away again, I'd offer to help." Clementine had a righteous look on her features. "But I know better now."

"You sent her away?" Lawrence's tone was incredulous. For the first time, his gaze held no familiar spark of admiration.

"We asked her to help gather greens." Nessa gaped at the other woman. How dare she imply that they'd excluded her!

"A fool's errand." Clementine reached into her apron pocket and produced a handful of grass. "No one would actually cook this!"

"Those aren't dandelion greens," Nessa all but snapped. "And we do use those."

"Dandelions are good for lots of things." Isaac stepped forward, away from Clementine. "Fried blossoms, salads... Nessa wouldn't send you on a wild goose chase."

"How was I to know?" The woman put her hands on her hips. "It sounded ridiculous."

"I've never heard of eating dandelions," her brother mused. "But if Nessa asked you to pick a few, you should have trusted her judgment."

"Thank you." Nessa chose not to point out that Lawrence hadn't trusted her a moment ago. Isaac had. As she walked back to the cook fire, Nessa wondered whether or not that was significant.

Lord, I came here in hopes that You'd reveal Your plan to me. So how is it that I constantly feel as though I'm walking in circles?

fifteen

"You could've knocked me over with a feather when I tasted that dinner," Clementine trilled as they got under way once more. "Who would've imagined dandelion leaves with pork and potatoes would be such a tasty dish?"

"Nessa, Mrs. MacLean, and I did." Julia's dry tone made Isaac grin. "It's why we asked you to help gather the greens."

"You'll have to forgive me for thinking you were having a little joke at my expense."

"In all the years I've known them, Julia, Nessa, and Mrs. MacLean have never ill-used anyone." Michael sounded loud in the closed car. "It's an insult to all three that you would imagine otherwise."

"A simple misunderstanding, that's all it was." Clementine toyed with the fingers of her kid leather gloves.

"Admitting you were wrong is a step in the right direction." Isaac slowed to take a curve. "Apologizing for misjudging the other women is another."

"Apologize!" Clementine sniffed. "When I've done nothing wrong? Believe me, no one saw fit to inform me that I'd be expected to pick weeds and cook on this vacation. As far as I'm concerned, I offered to help. That's all there is to it."

"No." Michael's harsh tone belied his even words. "Helping is a way of life out here, not deserving of any particular credit."

"Well, I never!"

"Perhaps you should." Isaac frowned but resisted the urge to shift his gaze from the road. "We men do the driving, look after the cars, carry the luggage, and oversee the arrangements. Nessa, Julia, and Mrs. MacLean packed provisions for the trip and are quick to lend a hand or prepare a meal. We all do our parts."

"Isaac," she placed a beseeching hand on his shoulder as she entreated, "surely you see that I only wanted to help. I never meant to give offense."

"I know." Some of his ire dissipated. "But by implying that the others were treating you poorly, you did insult them. I know a soft heart like yours wouldn't want to leave it like that."

"You're right." She shifted in her seat. "Julia, I'm sorry. And I'll tell the others at our next stop."

"Thank you." Julia sounded more relaxed. "We'll all appreciate that."

The rest of the drive passed amicably, but Isaac stayed silent. Clementine's behavior bothered him, but he couldn't pin down the reason why. It wasn't fair to compare her to Nessa, who'd grown up working alongside her mother and her grandmother. Clementine was gently reared, housed at a finishing school where she learned to manage a household—not the day-to-day upkeep. He'd thought she would learn what was needed to survive and run a family. For the first time, he wondered if she was willing to put in that kind of work.

He shook the doubts from his mind as they pulled up to the Main Terrace, which featured incredible plateaus of deposited limestone. While Isaac set up his camera, he was pleased to see Clementine talking to Nessa and Mrs. MacLean, obviously apologizing for her unintended rude remarks. He was thrilled as he snapped what should be a wonderful shot of the Bethesda Geyser.

"I'm surprised there aren't bathers here, as well." Lawrence flipped through the guide as Nessa joined them. "Says here that it's particularly known for its healing waters. Someone commented, 'The Angel of Health is continually stirring the waters.'"

"Must be why this particular part is called Angel Terrace." Nessa scooted close to Lawrence, looking at the pamphlet. "Whatever the reason, you must be glad of the chance to photograph the geyser without jostling other tourists."

"True." Isaac relished that small smile, one of the precious few he'd enjoyed for the past five weeks.

Isaac was still smiling when he secured his photography case and they passed through Yellowstone's Golden Gate. According to the blurb Michael read, the gold-colored lichens on the walls of the short canyons were the cause for the park's name.

"So unusual," Julia marveled.

They appreciated the view in silence until they came to a place where the shoulder of the road was widened and they could pull off. The muted roar of a waterfall lured them out of the automobiles.

"I can't see it." Clementine rose to her tiptoes as she spoke for the first time since her apology.

"Let's follow the path." Lawrence offered Nessa his arm. They led the way, everyone falling into place behind them.

Isaac sought out Clementine, regretting that she was so hard struck by his earlier disapproval. Her bright smile went a long way toward easing his doubts.

Clementine Hepplewhite might have been a sheltered young girl, but she was growing into an intriguing—not to mention beautiful—woman.

❧

"There!" Nessa leaned forward to get a better view through the slatted windshield. "That's got to be Electric Peak! I'm almost sorry we decided not to try traversing it."

"The roads only go so far," Lawrence reminded her. "And though it doesn't look so imposing from here, it's almost eleven thousand feet high."

"That's why she said 'almost,'" Grandmam pointed out. "If Nessa had her heart set on making it to the top of that mountain, not even rain could stop her."

"She's an intrepid woman." Lawrence's indulgent smile made Nessa feel more like a wayward child than a courageous explorer.

"Rain is the one thing that would certainly stop me from attempting Electric Peak, Grandmam." Nessa read aloud, "'It was named by Hayden Survey topographers from their 'hair-raising' experience involving electricity on top of the mountain.'"

"Sounds dangerous." Lawrence bore down on the gas pedal as though eager to make a quick escape.

"It was. One Henry Gannett ascended the mountain in 1872, only to be struck by lightning. Happened to his follower, too." Nessa shivered. "I'm glad to say that they both survived. Escaped with tingles, singed hair, and ruined clothing."

Grandmam added, "I'm sorry to say it, but they had no business going to high ground during a thunderstorm."

"Agreed." Lawrence cleared his throat. "Does that guide say anything about other areas where unsuspecting explorers might be electrocuted?"

"Not that I see." Nessa turned the pamphlet over. "Though it does mention that the incident happened in July. They probably never anticipated a thunderstorm."

"Looks like we've made it to the campsite." Lawrence made a shallow turn westward, following Isaac's lead. "The trees are thinning out."

"Look at all those blue-striped tents." Grandmam scooted

to the side for a better look. "Wait. Why is Isaac turning away from them?" Sure enough, he was following a small side road.

"The blue-striped tents belong to the Wylie Camping Company," Lawrence explained. "We've made arrangements with Shaw and Powell."

In a few moments, they pulled up near a rustic wooden structure bustling with activity. A large sign proclaimed DINING HALL.

Before too long, they were led to their tents—on foot. The automobiles couldn't come any closer, the man explained, on account of no roads and problems with spooking their horses. Shaw and Powell ran a tour with horse-drawn Studebaker coaches.

"Remember that your group needs to leave a goodly ways before we do," the man cautioned as he stopped before two tents. "That way we'll be far enough apart so the horses don't spook and we won't have any nasty problems."

"I take it you've already had some problems since the park began admitting automobiles?" Isaac thrust his hands in his pockets at the man's emphatic nod. "We'll be on our way directly after breakfast, then."

"I appreciate that." He shook Isaac's hand then disappeared into the village of tents blanketing the ground.

"We'll go get the luggage." Lawrence undid the top button of his coat.

"Thank you." Clementine opened the flap of the first tent and ducked inside. After a scant moment, she emerged and headed for the second.

Nessa and Julia shared a disbelieving glance as Clementine poked her head through the opening.

"They're exactly the same!" Distress rang in her pronouncement. She marched outside carrying a stack of blankets.

"We'll all freeze tonight."

"What are you doing?" Grandmam gave voice to the question on everyone's mind.

"While the men fetch our luggage, they'll have to see about getting more blankets." She hugged the bundle close to her chest. "Obviously someone needs to take things in hand. The management of this. . .place. . .leaves much to be desired."

"It's a campground." Julia stated what was obvious to the rest of them. "It's not a resort."

"That doesn't mean we should lower our standards," Clementine insisted.

"Nor do we demand special treatment from a facility that has already made special arrangements for us." Isaac's furrowed brow made Clementine's lip tremble.

"I brought my winter cloak, so if you're cold, you can use one of my blankets." Nessa gently took the pile from Clementine and returned it to the second tent.

"But. . .we'll be cold. And in tents." Clementine looked at the ground as she whispered, "What if bears come?"

An unexpected wave of sympathy coursed through Nessa. Clementine's demands were all false bravado. Deep down, she was just afraid of the unfamiliar.

"We'll be fine." Isaac tucked her in the crook of his arm, and Nessa's sympathy ebbed. "The campfires will keep the wildlife away, and the tents are only for one night. Besides, we'll be in the tent right next to you if you need us."

"Exactly." Lawrence drew Nessa close as though she, too, needed comforting.

Watching Isaac with Clementine, Nessa began to think she just might.

sixteen

"What's that?" Clementine screeched as something moved in the trees beside the road.

Isaac eased off the gas and hit the brake pedal, causing the car to chuff to a halt. Behind him, Lawrence did the same. Both Fords came to a stop a ways from where the heavy shadow lumbered in the woods.

"It could be a bear!" Clementine hastily rolled up her window. "Why would you stop?"

"The creature had antlers," Julia soothed. "It wasn't a bear. Probably an elk or a moose. Don't you want to see it?" Not waiting for an answer, she stepped out of the car, Michael on her heels.

"Come with us." Isaac had already exited the vehicle and stood beside Clementine's door.

"Why do you want to see it?" She reluctantly took his hand. "Don't you usually shoot deer and things with antlers? Why marvel at one now?"

"Sometimes it's good to look at something from a new perspective." Nessa came around the back of the touring car. "It's a moose!"

"Huge one, too." Lawrence came beside Nessa.

I should have known he'd pop up wherever Nessa went. Isaac grimaced.

"Is it safe?" Clementine clung to his arm but looked at Lawrence.

"If Mrs. MacLean isn't afraid to get an up-close look, I'd

say so." Her brother grinned. "Though she's one woman in a million."

"We like to think so." Nessa beamed up at him.

"You missed it!" The rest of their group hurried back.

"Oh well, I'll just have to catch the next one." Clementine hopped back into the car and swung the door shut.

"I've never seen one so big," Michael described. "The antlers were as long as my arm."

"What about it's nose?" Julia rubbed her own.

"Sounds like a moose all right." Isaac finished winding the crank, and the rest of them climbed inside the vehicles. "They're supposed to like willows, and there are a lot of those in this area."

They kept going at a leisurely pace, taking in the sights around them. A small creek alongside the road displayed on odd greenish-yellow tinge to the water, causing Julia to consult the pamphlet.

"This must be Lemonade Creek," she decided. "Called that because of its yellow color. Some guides claim to carry sacks of sugar to add to the water so they can serve some to the tourists."

"I love lemonade!" Clementine peeped out the window. "But I don't see how there can be a creek full of lemon juice."

"It's not." Isaac grinned. "You'll notice the pamphlet didn't actually advise drinking the water. Must be caused by minerals or such from all the hot springs."

"Oh." Disappointed, she sank back onto the padded seat.

He kept driving, passing a rock face full of smooth black shards of what the guide said was volcanic glass. The area was called Obsidian Cliff. The creek running through went by the same name. The black glass caught the sunlight, reflecting patches of yellow light so that the water seemed to dance.

Isaac decided to bypass Clearwater Springs, which was labeled as dangerous. Apparently, visitors regularly didn't heed the warning signs, moving too far on the thin crust of earth covering the heat below. None of them fancied getting burned when they'd already seen Mammoth and Bethesda springs, so they admired the pockmarked landscape from within the safety of the Fords.

They didn't get out to stretch their legs until reaching Frying Pan Spring. The large spring spread out on both sides of the road—the most unusual body of water Isaac had ever seen.

"Is it boiling?" Mrs. MacLean reached a hand high over the bubbling water. "Why is there no steam?"

"I don't know." Nessa stared at the surface of the water. "It looks like hot grease sputtering on a griddle, but it should be giving off a lot of heat if that were the case."

"The man from Shaw and Powell said you could boil an egg in under a minute." Lawrence pried open the crate and pulled one out. "Anyone care to test the theory?"

"Use this." Julia passed him a ladle so he wouldn't touch the surface of the water. "Just in case."

Everyone watched in silence as Lawrence placed the egg in the bowl of the ladle and cautiously lowered it until the entire egg was submerged in the bubbling water. The minute seemed to stretch out as they waited for the results.

"If the handle of that ladle isn't getting warm," Kaitlin MacLean advised, "then the water's not hot."

"Not heated at all." Lawrence drew the ladle and egg out of the water. He put out a cautious finger to give the shell a single, swift tap. "It's cold!" The affront in his voice made it hard for Isaac to hide his amusement.

"Guess you were taken in," he observed.

"I don't blame you." Nessa took the ladle, replacing it and the egg as she spoke. "What Isaac doesn't understand is that sometimes you hope for success in spite of evidence to the contrary."

☙

"I like what you said back there." Lawrence snuck a quick glance at her before returning his attention to the road. "Made me wonder though. What is it you hope for, Nessa?"

"A lot of different things. I'm not sure I could pin them all down to describe them." She gazed out the window at lush thickets of bristling evergreens.

"It'll be a little while until we stop again." He didn't push any further, just left Nessa feeling as though it might help her sort out her thoughts to have him listen.

"A loving marriage, a happy family, staying close to the people I love..." She shrugged. "The same as any other girl, I'd suppose." *Except that I wanted to share all of that with Isaac. Now that's looking less and less likely.*

"Sounds like the same things everyone wants." He darted another glance at Nessa. "Women and men alike."

"I hope so," Grandmam chimed in. "It takes one of each to make a marriage!"

"So it does." Lawrence adjusted the windshields. "Looks like we're coming to a stop."

Sure enough, Isaac's car was slowing toward an offshoot. The sign proclaimed Hazle Lake.

"They misspelled Hazel, unless it was intentional." Nessa puzzled over this until Grandmam explained that an early park tour guide had named the lake, and the misspelling stuck.

Nessa looked out over the water, which displayed an unusual color combination of amber and green. The sunlight danced on the water's movement, making the peaks of lazy waves glint gold. She'd never seen the color of her eyes reflected so completely.

"What an ugly lake." Clementine's pronouncement robbed Nessa of her smile. "All brown and brackish."

"It does seem very muddy," Lawrence agreed. "As though a lot of silt and dirt swirls around inside. Not the most pleasant view we've seen."

"I disagree." Isaac's firm declaration distracted Nessa from Lawrence's inadvertent insult. "One moment it looks green, another warm brown. And see how the sun plays on the surface, sending sparkles scattering across the water?" He stared into Nessa's eyes as he spoke, letting her know he wasn't only speaking of the lake. "Hazle, however they spelled it, is the perfect description for its unique splendor."

"It just looks dirty to me." Clementine's comment couldn't dampen the glow Nessa felt spreading across her face.

Isaac's opinion was the only one that mattered. She didn't say anything as they went back to the cars and drove on to the next wonder Yellowstone protected.

"Beryl Spring." Lawrence shouldered his way through another group of tourists. "Now this is worth stopping for!"

Nessa waited until a space opened then stepped forward to view the hot spring. The blue-green water gave off a hazy steam, showing why it had been named for an aqua gemstone.

"A man could get lost in those depths." Michael's ardent tone caused Nessa to turn to her right. He stood with his arm looped casually about her best friend's waist, looking deeply into Julia's eyes. "Pure color layered over deep mystery."

Julia blushed but never looked away from the man speaking such sweet words. Her friend, Nessa realized, had progressed from an unspoken crush to being completely enamored.

Which is well and good, because the man she admires looks back at her with the same soft gaze.

Against her most stringent determination not to, Nessa found herself looking at Isaac. *Here's to hoping. . .*

seventeen

The day seemed to fly by; none of the tensions from the previous day seemed to be dampening anyone's spirits. Aside from Clementine's fear of moose and Lawrence's dunderheaded comment about not appreciating Hazle Lake, Isaac would say that today was going very well.

They stopped for a lunch of beans 'n' bacon, which Clementine crumbled the bacon for.

As everyone finished the meal, Isaac brought up the prospect of taking a side loop road. "It's a one-way scenic trip, less than two miles," he explained. "Follows the Firehole River to Firehole Falls then rejoins the main road at the Cascades. Anybody interested?"

"Yes, please!" Nessa swiftly began cleaning up. "I don't know what it is about waterfalls, but I've never seen one I didn't fall completely in love with."

"That decides it then." Lawrence rose to his feet to help. "We can't stand in the path of love."

His comment made Nessa duck her head, depriving Isaac of seeing her reaction. *Just how serious are they becoming?* A heavy weight settled in his chest, the anticipation of taking the detour evaporating.

"Is there any chance we might get blocked with someone coming up such a small road from the other direction?" Michael was giving the automobiles a measuring look. "The Fords will probably take up all the space if it's not much more than a horse trail."

116

"The road only goes one way." Isaac clapped his friend on the shoulder, surreptitiously glancing over to where Lawrence was helping Nessa into his car. "So nobody will get in our way."

"We won't get wet, will we?" Clementine joined them. "I didn't think to pack a slicker. I wonder what else I forgot."

"Not much, from the size of your portmanteau." Isaac smiled to soften the words. "I suspect you came prepared for just about everything."

"You might be right," she simpered. "Though I know we ladies wouldn't make it far without your help."

"And the trip wouldn't be half as rewarding without your company." Isaac took hold of her elbow and helped her into the car. Her fancy beaded reticule snagged on the door handle, causing him to have to disentangle the delicate strap.

Clementine inspected the small purse. "No damage done. You were so quick to save it!"

If there was one thing at which she excelled, Isaac decided, it was making a man feel that his efforts were appreciated. *Clementine wouldn't refuse a proposal and not explain why.* The thought caught him off guard, and he almost missed the turn off.

The side road hadn't been paved yet, so Isaac was careful to avoid the worst ruts. He was gratified to see Lawrence follow him around the pitfalls—Nessa and Mrs. MacLean were safe enough. He drove alongside the river, its water much clearer than any of the creeks they'd seen up until now.

"It's so peaceful," Julia murmured.

Everyone stayed fairly quiet, ostensibly just drinking in the still, undisturbed beauty. When the roaring of the falls pulsed loudly in his ears, Isaac decided to stop. If he kept driving, he wouldn't get the chance to truly appreciate the view. Neither, he realized, would Lawrence.

"Wonderful idea to walk toward the falls," Michael commended.

"Something about drawing closer, hearing the power of the water churning more and more loudly—it's like we're closing in on a hidden treasure." Nessa couldn't contain her enthusiasm, and Isaac felt as though she shared it with everybody else.

When they first viewed the falls, it was through a framework of pine branches. Falling from a height of forty feet, the water rushed over a rock ledge and stretched to reach the churning pool below.

Isaac immediately turned around and went back for his camera case. During the time it took him to set everything up, Michael had gone back for Julia's art case, and she settled on a flat stone, busily filling her sketchbook with black strokes. Somehow those lines captured the elegance and sense of motion evoked by the waterfall. Isaac couldn't wait to develop his photograph and see what the film had captured.

"Doesn't it make you want to pick your way to the pool at its base, throw off your shoes, and dip your toes in the water?" Nessa breathed a sigh of appreciation.

"Never." Clementine's shocked gasp leeched some of the color from Nessa's cheeks. "Such a trek would absolutely ruin my skirts. And who knows what poisonous plants lay there!"

"It's not for everyone," Isaac placated. He shared a glance with Nessa. "But I know I would be tempted to try it."

"Not today!" Lawrence brushed a fly from his shoulder. "We'd best get back on the road so we make it to the Fountain Hotel before dark. There are still the Cascades to see today."

Isaac flipped the clasps on his photography case shut. He couldn't resist one last glimpse of the falls before he left. When he turned around, he saw that Nessa had done the same. She must have felt his gaze upon her, because she looked right at him. The same wistful admiration she'd bestowed on the falls stayed in her eyes as their eyes locked. She looked as though she was saying farewell to their long friendship, just as she had the water behind him.

Oh no, Nessa, he tried to convey in silence. *Don't think you're abandoning me in your past the way you're leaving this waterfall behind. We're not through yet.*

❧

The intensity in Isaac's gaze haunted Nessa long into the day. The tumbling fury of the Cascades pounding out a fierce rhythm seemed to seep into her skull as she tried to decipher the message he'd given her. But just like the dancing, foam-flecked water, she kept running up against the stones of confusion.

Her progress slowed, her purpose uncertain, she walked through the rest of the day like a shadow. Lawrence, seeming to sense that Nessa was grappling with something and wasn't her usual self, stayed close and supported her. He made conversation that didn't require more than the occasional nod or polite smile.

She'd seen that glint in Isaac's deep blue eyes often enough to recognize it as determination. All the same, she couldn't begin to guess what he was determined to do. What did it have to do with her?

He'd made it more than clear he was pursuing Clementine now. The petite blond perched next to him every moment of the drive to and through Yellowstone, with Isaac not making a single mention of how that relegated Nessa to Lawrence's vehicle.

God, I'm baffled by his behavior. If he has feelings for me, why didn't he show them before? Why in such a cryptic way now?

Lawrence is clear about his intentions—he's kind, attentive, and admiring. So why do my thoughts come back to Isaac again and again when he is so clearly taken with Clementine? I pray that by the end of this trip, You'll have given my heart the wisdom to make sense of it all.

Finally, Nessa drove the conundrum from her mind. If that one look had shown that God was working in Isaac's heart, so be it. If the Lord guided her to Lawrence, she'd follow. She'd made too many mistakes when she relied on her own emotions to trust them now. When they rolled to a stop, Nessa breathed a little easier. Everything was in God's hands.

CHRISTMAS TREE ROCK, the plaque read. She shaded her eyes and peered into the middle of Firehole River. There a large rock sprawled across the center of the softly rushing water. A single lodgepole pine stood straight and true, growing right out of the rock.

"I've never seen a tree grow through solid rock like that." Lawrence stared at it. "Incredible!"

"Must be an unusually strong tree," Nessa speculated, "to thrive despite the challenges it faces." *I wish I were strong enough to do the same.*

"Look at how the roots thrust right into the rock, taking what they need to keep the tree alive." Isaac was once again setting up his camera. "Now that's determination!"

"Is that all any of you sees when you look at this miracle?" Grandmam's eyes shone.

"The tree stands alone," Isaac replied. He glanced back at the unwavering center in the middle as though to be sure.

"No." Nessa suddenly understood what Grandmam was seeing. "The tree stands on the rock. The rock supports and gives life to the tree, even though the plant should be too weak."

"Exactly." Two tears rolled down Grandmam's face, causing Nessa to fold her arms around her. "It's just like us," she said. "The Lord is our rock and our salvation. Even though we're weak on our own, He sustains us."

"It's beautiful." Nessa felt as though it was an entirely new sight that lay before her, bathed in the beauty of love.

"Since my Arthur died," Grandmam sniffed, "I've struggled with feeling alone. That tree reminds me that God is always with me. That's what I see."

Isaac came out from behind his camera. "That's what everyone should see." He replaced Nessa, hugging Grandmam in the all-enveloping way only a man can hold a beloved old woman. "Thank you for showing us."

eighteen

"I wanted to catch a word with you." Michael found Isaac wiping dust off the windshields of his car. "Without anyone to overhear us."

"Sounds serious," Isaac teased. One look at his friend's face sobered him up. "Where is everyone else?"

"Looking for Clementine's lost earring." Michael gave a fleeting grin. "So there are five people in that hotel room, crawling around the floor in hopes of finding a lonely garnet."

"I don't see how that's funny." Isaac's brow knit. "It might be an heirloom or a treasured gift from her father."

"Julia swiped it." Michael gave a wink. "To give us some time to talk. She'll 'find' it in a little while."

"So what do you need to say?" Isaac leaned against the Ford, swiping at his boots with the dust cloth.

"Since we're stuck in the backseat with you and Clementine this whole trip," Michael began, "we can't help but notice you and she seem to be hitting it off, so to speak."

"Stuck?" Isaac raised his brows in mock affront.

"You know what I mean." Michael looked at the Ford.

"All right, all right. Yeah, we've been spending a lot of time together." He shrugged. "Nessa and Mrs. MacLean have been more than content to ride with Lawrence in the open-air runabout."

"True, but even when we're out of the car, it seems Clementine's vying with your sleeve just about every time we turn around. She hangs on your arm that much."

"The ground's less than steady, and her shoes weren't the best choice for exploring." Isaac wouldn't mention his suspicion that Clementine's vision wasn't as good as it seemed.

"Julia thinks Clementine might need spectacles," Michael commented. "So we were wondering if you'd noticed the same thing and were being a good Christian brother. . .or if it went deeper than that."

"I noticed," Isaac admitted. He wasn't betraying any secrets now that Michael had brought it up. "She needs support on the uneven paths. I also can't help but notice what a lovely young woman she is and how she appreciates the courtesy I show her. There's something appealing about being needed."

"And you think Nessa doesn't need you?" His friend tilted his head as though working out a kink. "Is that the problem?"

"The problem," Isaac spoke as clearly as possible, "is that Nessa rejected my proposal. She doesn't want to marry me."

"I wouldn't be so sure about that." Michael gave him a slanted look, as though he were privy to secret information.

"What did Julia tell you?" In spite of himself, Isaac stopped leaning on the car, standing at attention.

"Nothing I'm able to repeat. But I will say that neither Julia nor I nor Nessa feels that Clementine is a good match for you."

"Nessa doesn't have the right to judge who is or isn't a good match for me." Isaac slapped his hat on his head. "Not when she turned me down and still hasn't explained why."

"Is it that she hasn't explained"—Michael crossed his arms over his chest and glowered as he finished—"or that you weren't really listening to what she had to say about what she needs?"

"She hasn't explained." He bit off the sour words.

"Leave off thinking about Nessa for a moment." Michael

shoved aside the topic and plowed ahead. "Do you see Clementine as a potential wife? Are you courting her in earnest?"

"To an extent. A man could do far worse than to have a woman like Clementine on his arm." Isaac straightened his hat. "She's pretty, God-fearing, appreciative, honest to a fault. . ."

"To a fault." Michael latched onto that last phrase. "Have you noticed that she speaks without realizing the impact of her words? Like two days ago when she intimated that the other women were excluding her, making fun of her?"

"It's what she perceived to be the truth." Isaac remembered how woebegone she'd looked as she'd apologized. "Admitting a mistake and apologizing for it will stick in anyone's craw, but she did it anyway. She's even started helping where she can."

"That's another thing, Isaac. How can Clementine help you build a home and a family? She dresses well and moves gracefully, but can you honestly see her doing a lick of hard work?"

"She hasn't had to," he defended. "Clementine might have come into things later than Julia or Nessa, but she'll learn."

"If she wants to." Michael spoke in a low tone as everyone poured out the doors of the Fountain Hotel. "Are you even sure about that? Just think about it, Isaac."

"I will." He jerked the doors open. "And I expect you to support whatever decision I come to."

❧

"We saw geysers erupting from our bedroom window," Nessa mentioned. "Did you see the same thing?"

"Can't say we saw geysers erupting from your window." Lawrence shook his head in a fair imitation of regret. "The hotel didn't see fit to equip our rooms so. From our vantage point it looked like they were coming from the Lower Geyser Basin."

"You knew what I meant!" Nessa laughed at his mischievous smile. "Good to hear you spotted a few geysers yourself, though I would have been thrilled if the Excelsior had gone off. It's supposed to blast to a height of three hundred feet!"

"You know it hasn't had a documented eruption for over fifteen years." Grandmam clicked her tongue. "Don't you think we've already seen more than enough wonders to have justified this entire trip? I've already made many memories."

"As have I." Lawrence tightened his grip on the steering wheel. "You're in every last one, Nessa."

"You do have a way around a compliment, boy," Grandmam said approvingly from the backseat. "One would think the two of you have been alone instead of part of a large group."

Lawrence lowered his voice so the wind carried his words only to Nessa's ears. "Maybe sometimes it just feels that way."

"It's easy to lose oneself in awe of the sights we've seen." She deflected the compliment and steered the conversation to safer ground. "Which has been your favorite so far?"

"Which has been yours?" He glanced at her out of the corner of his eyes.

"Each is so unique, I'd be hard-pressed to choose just one." Nessa propped her arm on the windowsill. "That would be like choosing a favorite dish or a favorite person!"

"Sometimes we come across something so special, the choice is easy." Lawrence tried to catch her eye, but Nessa looked away and busied herself with looking out the window.

"Mine was the Christmas Tree Rock." Grandmam eased the silence. "Such a powerful reminder of God's love will always be precious to me. I'll hold it close for years to come."

"I think I would choose the same," Nessa agreed. "Not only

because of that reminder, which would be enough on its own, but for the joy it brought you." She reached across the back of the seat to clasp her grandmother's hand.

"The tree is an example to us all." This time Lawrence caught her eye as she turned back around. "With enough determination, we can conquer even the most difficult circumstances and achieve our goals."

"Is Isaac slowing down?" Nessa strove to keep her tone casual, ignoring the flush of heat she knew made her cheeks glow. It would be far too easy to lose her head over Lawrence's kind attentions and fulsome words. She'd only known the man for a few weeks, and he'd given her more compliments than Isaac had managed in an entire lifetime!

Slightly uneasy at the thought of further encouraging Lawrence when she wasn't certain of her feelings for Isaac, she climbed out of the car without waiting for him to get the door. His puzzled expression as he passed her to help Grandmam made Nessa wince. She hadn't meant to make it so obvious that she wanted to distance herself.

She gave him a bright smile to compensate for her rudeness, exclaiming, "I can't wait to see this. The Grand Prismatic Spring—doesn't it just sound mysterious and lovely all at the same time?" Nessa allowed him to place her hand in the crook of one arm, as he already escorted Grandmam with the other.

"Mysterious and lovely," Lawrence echoed, his gaze resting on her face. "An intriguing combination, to be sure."

Nessa's discomfort fled as she caught a glimpse of the spring. Steam rolled off the surface of the water in a filmy vapor. It seemed mystical, as though this spring had existed since the dawn of time, softly warming the air through ages until humans finally discovered its enchanting beauty.

"There!" An unfamiliar woman pointed high above the

spring, where the misty steam thinned and spread.

Nessa looked up and caught her breath at the shimmering light of an almost translucent rainbow. It quivered, suspended in the air by light and water, ebbing and flowing like a living thing. She stared at the phenomenon until it, much like the steam itself, evaporated into the air above.

"So that's why it's named after a prism." Lawrence shifted so that his hands rested on her shoulders. "It captures and reflects light in the same way as fine-cut crystal."

"The rainbow is a promise," Nessa said, remembering the story of Noah's flood. "A covenant between the Lord and Noah that He'd never again send a flood to destroy mankind. I've always thought how fitting a symbol it was."

"Because it uses water and light?" Lawrence sounded puzzled.

"No." She turned, gently shaking his hands from her shoulders. "It's symbolic of a promise because it's delicate, temporary, and meaningful only so long as those who see it honor God's will. It can't be captured or destroyed. It has to be believed in completely."

"That's beautiful." He reached down and took her hands in his, not meeting her gaze as he added, "It sounds a lot like love."

nineteen

"Biscuit Basin—they got the name right, that's for sure." Isaac scanned the area, noting the rock formations that looked a lot like, well, biscuits.

"Just like a man to notice something that resembles food." Clementine tapped his arm with the ivory fan she'd pulled out of her reticule. Then she snapped it open and languidly waved it before her face for a little while.

"So I take it your attention was caught by the Sapphire Pool?" Isaac raised his brows in silent challenge.

"Absolutely. The color is incredible!" She busied herself with tucking the fan into the small beaded bag. Though Isaac wouldn't have thought it possible, the thing fit.

"How like a woman to notice something named after a jewel." He closed the trap with a satisfied smile. His grin grew as everyone save Clementine burst into laughter.

"He's got you there, sis," Lawrence all but hooted.

"Now, wait a minute, Isaac Freimont!" Nessa shook her forefinger at him. "I noticed the biscuit-shaped rocks before admiring the sapphire pool. What do you make of that?"

"You're the exception." The retort softened into a compliment as he spoke it aloud. "A rarity among women."

"My thoughts exactly." Lawrence brushed a soft tendril behind Nessa's ear in a purely possessive motion.

"Thank you." Nessa fingered the errant strand. "Both of you." It gratified Isaac to no end to see that saucy little curl spring right back to caress her temple.

"We should be getting on," Lawrence said, clearing his throat and tossing Isaac a dark glower, "since we want to see the Hillside Springs before stopping for dinner."

"Fair enough." Isaac looked down as Clementine's cool hand snaked around his elbow. "Let's return to the automobiles."

As the day wore on, Clementine's idle chatter began to grate on Isaac's patience. She talked about her clothes, her jewelry, the parties she'd been to, the lovely vacations she'd had, the classes she'd taken at finishing school, and on and on until Isaac felt his temples throbbing. When did Clementine become so garrulous?

He resolved to find an open area for lunch close to Hillside Springs, if for no other reason than to escape her recitation for a few moments. From the amount of shifting Michael was doing behind him—Isaac could feel it every time his friend's knees hit the back of his seat—Isaac wasn't the only one who looked forward to some peace.

At Hillside Springs, it was with great reluctance that he helped Clementine out of the Ford. The little hands whose clasp he'd found sweet suddenly seemed like small, cold vises. As she gave a cry of distress over a tiny mud puddle, he wondered how he'd ever admired her fancy getups.

What sane woman traipsed around a forest in high-heeled boots, lace gloves, and satin gowns, carrying delicate purses? Isaac shut his eyes when she whipped out her fan once more. He hadn't even thought of the expensive earrings she'd left lying on a table in her hotel room. Was all this because she hadn't had enough time to order suitable clothing or because she didn't want to?

Michael's concern has me chewing over some things I wouldn't look at too closely before. Am I mirroring his doubts, or am I taking off my blinders? Give me wisdom, Lord.

Lawrence, Nessa, and Mrs. MacLean somehow beat them to the springs, and Isaac couldn't help but notice Nessa looked mighty pretty in her light, rose-colored cotton and sensible half boots. She'd forgotten her hat—again—and the sun practically danced on the opportunity to glisten in the deep red strands of her riotous curls. He drank in the view until Lawrence spotted him looking and placed his arm around Nessa's trim waist.

That man is getting too close for comfort.

"How strange!" Clementine's exclamation had him looking at the sight they'd stopped to appreciate.

"It's red." He couldn't quite keep the astonishment from his voice as he looked at the shocking color of the springs before him. Thankfully, the red had none of the purplish black undertones of blood.

"Tomato Soup Springs," Julia read from her ever-present pamphlet. She wasn't one to ever leave literature behind. "I'd say the reason for the nickname is pretty obvious."

"Biscuit Basin and Tomato Soup Springs." Isaac pulled his arm away from Clementine and rubbed his stomach. "Sounds like lunch to me! Is anybody else ready to stop and eat?"

"Yes!" Michael and Julia spoke as one, looked at each other in surprise, and shared a delighted smile. Obviously, Isaac wasn't the only one who wanted a reprieve from Clementine.

More than all the words she'd spewed, that simple fact spoke volumes.

❧

"Let's see if it works!" Nessa edged closer to Handkerchief Pool.

"Wait." Lawrence caught her by the arm. "The ground could be thin, or you might get burned. I'll make sure it's safe." With that, he nudged ahead of Nessa to block her way.

"It would have been fine," she muttered under her breath. Why Lawrence decided to treat her like a child was beyond understanding. She could make her own decisions, and it was on the tip of her tongue to tell him so when he whipped out a large white handkerchief, reached above the opening of the pool, and let go.

"Oh!" Everyone let loose excited gasps as the anomaly sucked in the clean linen, only to spit it back out freshly steamed. The handkerchief was tossed high in the air, allowing Lawrence to catch it neatly.

"Would you look at that," he marveled. "Something in that guide was actually true!"

"It's not fair to blame the guide because Frying Pan Lake didn't boil your egg," Grandmam chided. "It only said that it was a story the guides sometimes told."

"Well, it didn't mention that the story was false," Lawrence grumbled. "But this Handkerchief Pool is real enough!"

"I'd like to try it!" Clementine's excitement caused Isaac to lead her up to the spring—ahead of Nessa, who bit her lip so she didn't childishly demand that it was her turn.

In the end everyone enjoyed the sport, leaving with smiles on their faces and damp hankies in their pockets as another group took their place. By then the sun was sinking low in the sky, so they drove straight on to the Old Faithful Inn.

Nessa couldn't contain her smile at the "World's Largest Log Cabin," another Yellowstone claim to be taken with a grain of salt. All the same, it was a towering structure, about four stories tall, made almost entirely out of cut logs. The great doors were painted bright red, held in place with huge iron hinges, beckoning travelers to come inside.

"This is incredible!" Julia exclaimed as they entered the threshold. As with the basic structure, every bit of the interior was crafted from native logs, many of which hadn't been straightened but rather cunningly placed so that the angles or curves of the wood became decorative as well as functional.

They'd stepped into a large open space, filled with hardwood floors, wooden benches, and a massive stone fireplace stretching all the way to the ceiling. That drew Nessa's gaze upward, displaying the walkways guarded by rails that ringed around the open-area fireplace for two more stories.

"What's that?" Nessa tilted her head back to spy a room, set at the tallest point of the ceiling, the peak of the roof making the high room look like a small house.

"The crow's nest." Lawrence stood so close she could feel his breath tickling her escaped curls. "They keep it as an orchestra house; the music plays every night for the guests."

"Fascinating." She stepped away from him, using the pretext of inspecting the fireplace more closely. One side was open, but the other three housed great niches cut into the face of the stones, storage places for massive amounts of firewood.

"We're on the third floor." Isaac called. "Up those stairs." He gestured toward steps made of logs hewn lengthwise and stacked in the staggered pattern of a stairwell.

"Before we go up, do you think we can see Old Faithful spout off?" Clementine, as usual, clung to Isaac's arm. "It's supposed to be fairly regular."

"The hotel worker mentioned that, as best they could calculate, it would be due for another eruption in about ten minutes." Michael turned to Julia. "Would you like to see it in the glow of the sunset?"

Julia's cheeks glowed in a fair approximation as she nodded. By now it was obvious that Michael returned her interest. . . and was stealthily moving their courtship forward. The pair trooped outside, leaving everyone else to follow them out the door and up the gravel path that led to the famous geyser.

"Shall we?" Lawrence offered his arm with his customary flourish.

The gesture had charmed Nessa the first few times but was beginning to seem superfluous and overly formal. "Yes."

They walked the short distance, their group assembling as the little curls of steam rising from the ground began to grow larger, the transparent wisps darkening to white billows until the escalating rumble was drowned out by the *whoooosh* of water.

The first time the water pushed into the air, it didn't reach very high. Clementine was just voicing her disappointment when the action repeated, the eruption climbing taller. A rapid succession followed, each burst scaling greater heights, until a great hiss sounded and the water seemed to fly as high as the mountains in the background.

Nessa caught her breath, engrossed in the beauty before her. Water and steam danced high in the air, capturing the golden rose glow of the setting sun for a few playful moments. Then the eruptions slowed, grew smaller, and retreated back into the earth below.

twenty

"Do you think you got good pictures of the Kepler Cascades?" Clementine didn't stop talking long enough for Isaac to answer. "I thought they were amazing—a series of waterfalls. Who would have thought up something like that? Over a hundred feet!"

"God thought it up." Julia somehow managed to stay polite beneath the onslaught of Clementine's declarations. "Same as He created all the incredible things we've seen on this trip."

"Oh yes, of course!" And Clementine was off again.

Isaac focused on the road, trying to block out some of the noise by concocting outrageous schemes to make her ride in her brother's car for the duration of the trip. Aside from mutilating the Ford itself, which he refused to even contemplate despite the dire circumstances, he considered a range of options.

So far, the best of the lot was asking Julia to feign car sickness, the threat of which should have Clementine scrambling away as fast as she possibly could. The only hitch was the dishonesty of it, which ruined everything. Isaac entertained a few fleeting thoughts about whether Julia had ever had motion sickness in the past so a casual mention could be made. . . .

As they rounded a corner around Shoshone Lake, Michael cut through Clementine's litany. His friend manfully ignored the peevish glance she sent his way, instead gesturing to the pamphlet in his hand. "I thought you might like to know that this was the site of the last stagecoach holdup in Yellowstone."

He politely inquired, "Is anyone interested in hearing the details?"

"To tell the truth, I've never enjoyed stories about—"

"Yes!" Julia and Isaac drowned out what would surely have been another of Clementine's rambling stories.

"Seems one Edwin B. Trafton decided to emulate the Turtle Rock robbery of 1908." Michael spoke slowly, and Isaac knew his friend was trying to draw the story out.

God bless Michael, he prayed quickly before interrupting. "I don't remember everything about that incident. Could you remind me of the details?"

"Sure. In 1908 a robber—identity still unknown—held up a train of thirty stagecoaches at Turtle Rock. Accounts vary, saying he made off with one thousand to three thousand dollars he took from tourists. He was never caught."

"Gracious," Clementine breathed. Her gaze darted around the rocks bordering the road as she locked the door.

"So in 1914 a fellow by the name of Edwin Trafton decided that holding up tourists was a grand idea. He waited at Shoshone Point, held up fifteen coaches, and stole over nine hundred dollars—a good bit less than his predecessor."

"How was he caught?" Julia sounded puzzled.

"Seems he didn't realize the tourists thought it was all a part of the tour itself." Laughter tinged Michael's voice as he continued on. They snapped pictures of him to remember the incident, and the police used those to identify and capture him."

"What a foolish man!" Clementine cackled next to Isaac. "Some folks just don't know when to leave good enough alone." With that, she was off and running about the time when one of her friends did something similar.

As she prattled on, Isaac decided they'd need to stop for an even earlier lunch that day.

ð

"Who thinks we should send Clementine for the ham and have her cut slices of it while we bake the biscuits?" Nessa all but whispered the words, though she needn't have bothered. Clementine seemed as affixed to Isaac's side as ever, so she wouldn't overhear Nessa's scheming.

"She'll make them uneven," Grandmam fretted.

"But she'll be over there, using that great big stump," Julia pointed out. She gave a happy little sigh. "All the way over there."

"Let's ask Lawrence to help her," Nessa hurriedly added as she spotted him sauntering toward her. "So she won't cut herself or anything horrible like that."

"I'll make the arrangements." With a knowing glance, Grandmam bustled off. She did a fine job of catching Lawrence's arm and turning him toward Clementine, hands waving in the air as she described exactly what she needed him to do.

"The reasons why I want Clementine off in the distance is obvious," Julia remarked. "What has Lawrence done to earn exile?"

"I can't so much as scratch my nose without him offering me his handkerchief." Nessa knew she was grumbling, but she couldn't stem the tide. "Every time I turn around, he's opening a door or carrying my luggage or holding my elbow as though I can't walk without his support. He's driving me half mad."

"You wanted an attentive suitor," her friend observed. "Seems like Lawrence fits the bill quite nicely."

"He does not fit the bill." Nessa poured flour into the mixing bowl she'd set atop the egg crate. "He weaseled his way into the bill then stretched it all out of proportion. Oh, listen to me. Lawrence hasn't done a single thing wrong, and here I am, sniping over all his kindness." A wave of guilt swamped her.

"He's been a perfect gentleman."

"Maybe that's the problem." Julia handed her the salt. "Lawrence might just be a little too perfect. You've never been one to follow the rules as strictly as he seems to."

"You're a genius, you know that?" Nessa gave her friend a quick hug as Grandmam came back toward them. "I couldn't figure out what was bothering me, and you hit on it without even trying. Lawrence does need his feathers ruffled a little, and I might be just the woman to do it!"

"You've got that look again." Julia's smile disappeared, replaced by a look of caution. "Think about it carefully."

"How could it go wrong?" Nessa thought for a moment as she mixed the biscuit dough. "It's not as though I'd do something scandalous—just shake him out of his staid routine a little."

"If there's one thing I've learned after all the years of our friendship, it's that something can always go wrong."

"In what way could a little fun backfire?"

"What if Lawrence decides he needs to keep a closer watch on you to protect you from your impulsive shenanigans?" Julia helped shape the dough into biscuits then popped the first batch into the Dutch oven. "Could make him even more starchy."

"Oh no." Nessa wiped her hands on her apron. "He might react poorly and start to hover even more!"

"Lawrence?" Grandmam guessed. "He has been following you about like a babe in leading strings. You don't enjoy all the attention he gives you?"

"Some of it." Nessa blew a few wisps of hair from her forehead, venting her exasperation. "In the beginning, he made me feel special. The attention was flattering, not to mention a refreshing change from Isaac's obtuseness."

"So what changed?" Julia used the tongs to put more hot ashes atop the oven. "Or rather, who?"

"Who?" Nessa frowned. "You mean, did he become smothering or did I come to realize I didn't want to be smothered?" She waited for Julia's nod. "Both. He's latched on more tightly, and it's made me want to break free."

"You aren't bound to him, Nessa." Grandmam patted her arm.

"Exactly!" Nessa nodded eagerly. "Maybe that's why I chafe at the way he acts as though I am. He's starting to seem possessive, but I'm not a possession for him to claim."

"Your ma had the same problem with Isaac's brother, you know." Grandmam pulled the pan of fluffy biscuits from the Dutch oven. "Men claim women as their own as a way of showing they care."

"Here I thought it was to warn off other men," Nessa griped. She hadn't missed the way Isaac glowered at Lawrence.

"That, too." Grandmam laughed. "To men it's all part of the same thing. You, my dear, have to decide whom you'll allow to claim your heart."

twenty-one

Lord, how can it take no more than a couple of days and a few words from a well-meaning friend to reveal Clementine's shortcomings, when I've spent so much time hoping she'd make the perfect bride? I concentrated on bemoaning my responsibilities, reluctant to fulfill them. No more. Show me Your way, and I will take it.

"Looks like it's been a rough day for you." Michael flopped down on his bed. "Hope that's not because of our talk the other day." He spoke freely because Lawrence was out trying to find shoe polish, of all things, for his sister.

"Part of it is." Isaac pulled off his boots. "It made me take a long hard look at Clementine—past her pretty smiles."

"What did you see?"

"She's everything I ever thought I truly wanted in a wife."

"Is that so?" Michael tried to sound casual, but Isaac knew his friend had grave misgivings.

"Clementine is sweet, pretty, always has a ready smile, and makes a man want to protect her." Isaac smiled at the pained look on Michael's face. "Funny thing is. . .I was wrong."

"You had me worried for a minute there."

"Couldn't resist." He leaned back. "Clementine isn't a woman I'll ever be able to really talk to, spend my life with day in and day out. She can't keep a house or raise children, and she'd be miserable as a farmer's wife. It'll never work."

"So glad you realized that." Michael slapped his knee, a sly look crossing over his face. "Figure anything else out, while you were at it?"

"That's not so clear." Isaac rolled over, propping his head on his hand. "I realize now that Nessa isn't just the wife everyone expected me to take—she's the wife I should have always wanted." He thought he heard footsteps outside, but then a door opened and he put it from his mind.

"So what are you prepared to do about it?"

"I can't say. She rejected my proposal, and I'm still not certain why. That's a huge barrier, so I wonder if Nessa isn't the one for me but someone a lot more like her than Clementine ever will be. Could be I need to travel around, meet more women than Saddleback has to offer."

"You've come a long way for one day." Michael dropped his head onto the pillow. "So I'm going to leave it at being glad you're no longer considering Clementine."

"Exactly." Isaac shut his eyes. "Tomorrow I'll need to take Clementine aside and gently tell her the proposal she may be hoping for won't be coming."

"Wonderful to hear you've that much worked out."

"It's a start." Isaac unbent his knees, lying flat. "The rest will be clear sooner or later."

"So long as it's not too late," his friend muttered.

"What's that supposed to mean?" Isaac sat up as another floorboard creaked in the hall outside.

"How do you feel when Lawrence puts his arm around Nessa's waist? Or sticks to her side like a shadow?"

"Like I want to pry him off with a crowbar." Isaac tensed at the very thought. "He hovers around too close."

"Why should that bother you if it doesn't bother Nessa?"

"It shouldn't, but it does anyway." Isaac heaved a sigh. "Nessa may not have accepted my proposal, but that doesn't mean I'll quietly let her chain herself to Lawrence Hepplewhite."

The doorknob rattled as Lawrence let himself in. There was

no way to know how much he'd overheard, but from the forced cheerfulness in his face, Isaac suspected it had been everything since that first floorboard squeaked.

Sneakiness got added to the growing list of things Isaac didn't like about that man. Now what was he going to do about it?

❧

"Where are those two going?" Nessa watched as Isaac led Clementine under the relative privacy of a shady tree.

"Not far." Grandmam eyed the couple. "I'd be more concerned about what they were saying."

"Nessa?" Lawrence came up so quietly he made her give a little jump. "Can I have a word with you?"

"What is it?" She untied her apron strings.

"I meant in private." He offered her his arm, leaving her with no choice but to take it. Lawrence took her to a tree on the opposite side of the field, letting her sit on a flat rock eerily similar to the one she'd sat on while Isaac gave her that travesty of a proposal.

"Nessa, you know Isaac and I share a room with Michael. An interesting conversation took place last night, and I wanted to talk with you about it." He looked distinctly uncomfortable, his gaze shifting around as though he were reluctant to look at her.

"What is it, Lawrence?"

"I've noticed the looks that pass between you and Isaac sometimes but had hoped you might come to feel an abiding affection for me." He dropped to one knee. "Nessa, I want you to be my wife. I'll treasure you through the years to come, delight in our children, and strive to give you everything you've ever wanted. Wait." He put a finger to her lips, silencing her when she would have interrupted.

Since Nessa wasn't positive what she would have said, she

let him continue. The idea of refusing another proposal turned her stomach.

"But after last night, I'm more aware of your history with Isaac. I know he proposed to you, and I know you refused him."

How much did Isaac tell him? And why?

"I can see you have questions. Let me say that I don't know why you refused him, but it doesn't matter to me. All that matters is that you refused him and you're free to marry me."

"Lawrence, Isaac and I—" She paused, searching for words to explain what even she didn't fully understand.

"It's in the past." He gave a small, rueful smile. "I know you aren't in love with me yet, but I hope one day you'll look at me with the same admiration I feel for you."

"You're a really wonderful guy, but I don't think—"

"If you're worried about Isaac, I can assure you that he's moved on. He's done a lot of thinking these past few days, and he says Clementine is all he's ever truly wanted in a wife." He gave a slight nod in response to her surprise. "I know that he planned to have an important conversation with her today—something about a proposal."

"Now?" Nessa craned her neck, trying to look past Lawrence to where Clementine and Isaac were still alone together.

"I think so." He gave her a look of sympathy. "It's why I took you aside now, so you could be prepared. They probably won't announce anything today—it's only proper for a man to seek the blessing of the woman's father before saying anything. But I wanted you to know that you're. . .free."

"Free," she echoed, numb from the tightness in her chest.

"To marry me," he encouraged. "Don't answer now. Just think about it."

"Thank you for telling me." Nessa struggled to stand up. "It's a lot to think about."

twenty-two

I can't believe it, Lord! It's only been weeks since he proposed to me, and now he wants to marry someone else? I know I asked for You to make things clear, but I never imagined it would hurt so much.

Nessa all but ran through the forest until she couldn't see Lawrence anymore. Then she abandoned all pretense, leaned her back against a tree, wrapped her arms around her stomach, and sobbed. She took in great, shuddering gasps of air, but they all caught in her throat.

I knew he didn't love me, she tried to reason with herself, but the thought only made her cry harder. *But I hoped that maybe, somewhere deep inside, he did. Then he'd come to realize it, and we'd both be so happy. . .*

Her knees buckled as she sank to the ground, feeling the rough bark catch at the back of her dress as she scraped down, and not caring if it was ruined. She rested her head on her knees, holding her breath in a failed effort to stop the sobs.

What am I to do? The thoughts poured forth in tears. *Pretend I know nothing? Does Isaac really love her, Jesus? If so, am I to accept Lawrence's proposal, though I don't love him?*

Maybe. Her sobs faded into sniffles and hiccoughs. *Maybe I am supposed to marry Lawrence. I've chased love all my life, and look what it's brought me to. Lawrence won't be tricked—he knows I don't care for him as he cares for me. How do I know, Lord?*

And suddenly, she knew. She had to talk to Isaac. Nessa shakily rose to her feet, swiping the last tears from her face, breathing slowly until there was no sign of her sorrow. She brushed leaves from her dress, tidied her hair as best she could, straightened her shoulders, and walked back to find Isaac.

Her resolve wavered a moment when she saw he was still alone with Clementine, who was nodding and waving her arms in grand motions.

Probably planning the wedding ceremony. Nessa choked on the bitter thought but pressed forward. She didn't even look at anyone else, keeping her gaze fixed firmly ahead.

By the time she drew near, Clementine was leaving Isaac. Joy glinted in the other woman's pale blue eyes and smiling features, but Clementine didn't say a word—just gave a friendly little wave and veered off toward the cook fire. So they weren't announcing it yet, just as Lawrence predicted.

Nessa's step faltered for a moment, her fists clenching against the realization. Somehow, she kept going, though the look of surprise that flitted across his face didn't bode well. "How was your talk with Clementine?" She forced herself to sound casual but suspected she'd failed abysmally.

"Far better than I'd hoped." Satisfaction underwrote every word as he rocked back on his heels. "I did see you went off with Lawrence for a while." He stopped rocking. "Anything interesting happen?" His brow furrowed anxiously.

He knows. Just like he told Lawrence about his intentions toward Clementine, Lawrence admitted his own plans. Nessa tried to swallow the lump in her throat. *He hopes it went well so nothing will mar the success of his romance with Clementine.*

"He proposed to me." The words tumbled from her mouth before she could stop them.

"So soon?" Isaac blurted out, as though he had any room to judge. He'd known Clementine for precisely the same amount of time Lawrence had known her, after all!

"Yes." She looked away momentarily, closing her eyes against a fresh wave of grief.

"What did you say?" He stepped closer, obviously eager to hear that the woman he'd proposed to first wouldn't present a threat to his new engagement.

"I didn't answer him. Yet." She met his gaze defiantly, but her bravado sheered away as she saw the muscle in his jaw clench. "First I had to talk with you, Isaac."

"You think I'd stand in your way?"

I hoped so, her heart cried. "No. But I had to find out if you, that is, whether. . ." She couldn't seem to force the words out. Nessa took a deep breath and tried again "Whether the proposal was real. That you meant what you said to Clementine."

"A man doesn't propose lightly." Isaac's voice sounded tight, as though forced from his chest. "I meant everything I said, Nessa. You should know that."

"Are you absolutely sure?" She couldn't hold the words back, giving him one last chance to take her in his arms and prove that he loved her, not Clementine.

"When have you known me to make a decision in haste?" Isaac had a point, considering she'd waited for him for years before he came to the sticking point. And then they both got stuck there—until now.

"That's it then." She tried to act as though his revelation hadn't been a fatal blow. "I'm sorry to have ruined your plans, but it turns out to be for the best. You know I wish you every happiness." *Even at the cost of my own.*

"As I do for you." His breath came fast and shallow. "Goodbye, Nessa." With that, Isaac turned and stalked off, leaving her more alone than she'd ever been.

❧

"Aaaggghhh." Isaac unleashed an angry bellow and smashed

his fist into a nearby tree, scarcely noticing the scrape of the bark against his knuckles. The rage seeped from his chest to pulse in his aching hand, allowing him to breathe again.

"Did you know," Michael's voice reached Isaac before he saw his friend approach, "that an impressive number of birds took flight from just about the spot where you're standing?"

"No." Isaac growled the syllable, a short warning that should have his friend backing off.

"It's true." Michael moved closer, his gaze scanning the broken bark of the tree and flitting to Isaac's hand. "And I'm going to take a wild guess and say you're the cause for it."

"Mmh." Isaac grunted and looked at his hand. His knuckles had swollen, the scrapes on the back of his hand sluggishly oozing blood.

"It's enough to make a friend worry about how your conversation with Clementine went."

"Fine." He still wasn't sure he wanted to talk.

"How about you walk me through that then?" Michael cheerfully settled himself on a low branch.

"Go away," Isaac ground the words out. Now wasn't the time to discuss Clementine. Now was the time he needed to sort out his thoughts about Lawrence's proposal.

"No such luck." His friend shifted into a more comfortable position. "The last thing you need right now is to be left on your own." He gestured from Isaac's injured hand to the newly scarred tree. "Think of the damage you could do to our beloved national park with no one around to make you behave."

"Michael," Isaac gave up trying to intimidate his old friend, feeling the beginnings of a reluctant smile, "you should consider a career in politics."

"Nah. I'm too busy considering how to propose to Julia, then getting her to the altar and never letting her go. Love can do that to a man." Michael leaned forward. "But I think you already know that."

Isaac changed the subject. "Clementine took it well when I let her down. I told her she needed to consider what would really make her happy. . .and whether or not she'd find it in Saddleback. It didn't take long before her eyes lit up and she started nattering on about this fellow back in Charleston who'd proposed when he heard she was leaving."

"A fickle woman," his friend noted.

"She's not the only one." Isaac gave a short bark of laughter. "Nessa came to tell me Lawrence has proposed."

"No." Michael just about fell off his branch.

"Yes. But she hasn't answered him. . .yet." Isaac considered for a moment whether he'd do irreparable damage to his hand if he hit another tree. Or a rock.

"What?" was the most coherent thought his best friend managed.

"That sums it up." Isaac snorted. "Looks like that's God's answer—Nessa is going to marry Lawrence."

"You said she hadn't answered him."

"Yet." Isaac lowered himself to the ground but sprang up again to start pacing. "Nessa asked me if I'd really meant my proposal. Like she wanted me to tell her I wasn't serious so she could be free to run off with Lawrence and not feel guilty about it."

"That can't be right." Michael frowned. "We're missing something here."

"I told her I meant every word, and she apologized for ruining my plans. Said it all worked out for the best." Isaac cracked his knuckles and winced as pain shot up his arm.

"Maybe she thinks she's clearing the way for you and Clementine." Hope tinged the suggestion.

"Nope. She knew what I'd talked to Clementine about—asked how it went. When I told her it'd gone really well, that's when she started looking all hangdog and asked if I'd really meant the proposal." Isaac spared his hand and kicked a small rock, making it ricochet off a larger one with a loud *clunk*. "Nessa knew I still wanted her, and she felt bad because she's all set to marry Lawrence Hepplewhite."

"Isaac," his friend said slowly, as though turning his thoughts over to inspect the underside, "how would she know about what you said to Clementine?"

"I'm pretty sure Lawrence overheard us last night." Isaac kicked the larger rock, which didn't do more than scuffle a few inches. "Rotten sneak. Probably made me out to be some pitiful, lovesick boy when he talked to Nessa."

"I'm telling you," Michael protested, "I think something's not right here."

"That's true." Isaac shook his foot to alleviate the sting. "Nothing's turning out right."

twenty-three

The day wore on, hour after interminable hour. Nessa scarcely managed to scrape up enthusiasm for the Dragon's Mouth Spring, which normally would have made her delighted. The underground spring rushed up through a small hillside, emitting steam, and made rumbling, rasping sounds as though one of the mythical creatures crouched just inside the rocky overhang.

Since even this imagination-inspiring sight failed to chase away her doldrums, Nessa knew her heartsickness wouldn't be ebbing anytime soon. She kept her face turned during the drive, hoping that Lawrence would think she was enraptured by the majestic mountains and massive bison dotting the landscape. No sense making him feel as though his proposal depressed her.

They stopped at Rainy Lake, where the surface of the water rippled and ringed in little circles everywhere. Supposedly tiny springs beneath the surface disturbed the water, making it seem as though a perpetual rain fell above the lake. Nessa couldn't help but think that rain wasn't the only option—it would look the same if she stood in the middle and allowed herself to cry all the tears she held within.

The next few miles, they passed by Calcite Springs, and all pressed handkerchiefs or bandanas over their noses to ward away the offensive stench the land belched into the air. It smelled of rotten eggs and bitter medicine, strong enough to make everyone swallow back gags.

When they reached the hotel and the women were left in their room, Clementine hummed and slipped into a fresh dress, looking the very picture of a woman in love. Nessa couldn't remain silent for another moment. She had to be sure that if she was to bear the agony of a broken heart, Isaac's wife would love him as well as she.

"Do you love him?" The question came out more like a demand, but Nessa didn't bat an eyelash.

"What?" Clementine looked taken aback. In fact, she took a step away from Nessa. "I'm sure I don't know what you mean."

"It's simple." Nessa advanced a step as she spoke. "Isaac told me about your conversation today and the decision you reached. So I'm going to ask again, do you love him?" Her voice cracked. "You shouldn't marry him if you don't."

"Isaac told you?" Clementine's eyes narrowed; then she shrugged. "Well, to be honest, I hadn't thought so. I didn't realize it until today, as a matter of fact. How I could have taken him for granted for so long is beyond my understanding, but when I'm away from him—like now—I feel as though the best part of me has been ripped away. That must be love, right?"

"I suppose you'll have to wait to make it official." Nessa felt as though her entire body had gone numb.

"Yes, Daddy must be convinced that it's the right thing to do." Clementine shook the pins from her hair and picked up a silver-backed brush from her dresser set.

"That shouldn't be too hard." Nessa turned away, falling into a chair when she felt her legs would no longer support her weight.

"Maybe." She stroked her blond hair. "Maybe not, since I already told Daddy I didn't want to marry him."

"Why would you do a thing like that?" Nessa scarcely

noticed that Grandmam and Julia were hanging on their words, eyes wide as they drank in the conversation.

"Because he stutters and wheezes and is a little on the scrawny side. I never thought I could love someone who wasn't handsome, but there you have it."

"Isaac is handsome." Nessa sprang to her feet. "And he doesn't stutter at all!"

"I meant Charlie!" Clementine set her brush down with a thud. "He has breathing problems, that's all."

"Charlie?" Julia couldn't keep silent anymore. "Who's Charlie?"

"The man I want to marry." Clementine rolled her eyes. "At what point in this little talk did we start talking about Isaac?"

"You want to marry someone named Charlie?" Nessa echoed the words, wondering for a brief moment whether a good shaking would make Clementine speak sensibly.

"Yes. Charlie Peterson, from back home." Clementine's frown disappeared. "You thought Isaac and I were engaged? Whatever gave you that idea? He was very clear that he'd decided we wouldn't make a good couple when he spoke to me."

Nessa sat down again, abruptly. If Julia hadn't slid the chair behind her, she would have fallen to the ground in shock as she mentally relived what Isaac had told her that afternoon.

I had to find out if you, that is, whether. . .the proposal was real. That you meant what you said to Clementine? That was what she'd asked. She knew she'd specifically mentioned the proposal Lawrence assured her was coming. Isaac's response made no sense if he hadn't proposed.

A man doesn't propose lightly. I meant everything I said, Nessa. You should know that.

Unless. . .unless he'd thought she'd known he had broken it

off with Clementine and was telling her he'd meant what he'd said when he proposed to her!

Can it be that Isaac still wants to marry me?

⋙

Isaac put down the washcloth and tossed on his shirt as a loud knock sounded at the door. He moved quicker than Michael or Lawrence and opened it to find four women—and every one of them hopping mad.

"Isaac!" Nessa's scowl disappeared for a fleeting second before it returned with a vengeance. "Excuse me," she pushed past him and headed straight for Lawrence.

"What's going on?" Michael directed the question to Julia, but she shook her head and put a finger to her lips, obviously cautioning them not to interrupt.

"Hello, my love." Lawrence gave a ghost of a smile.

"Don't," Nessa spat out, jabbing him in the chest with her index finger with each word, "call me that, Lawrence Hepplewhite. You"—she gave an extra hard jab, judging by the wince it provoked, before she continued—"are a sneaking, rotten, no-good, dirty, rotten liar. How dare you!" She'd stopped jabbing with each word as she spoke more quickly, poking indiscriminately until Lawrence had backed up all the way to the wall.

"You said rotten twice." Isaac leaned back to enjoy the show. He didn't know what Lawrence had done to get Nessa all het up, but it must've been a humdinger. She'd never been this angry in all the years he'd know her.

"I know." Nessa didn't even turn around. "That's because he's really"—she started jabbing again at this point—"really rotten!"

"What is it, Nessa?" Lawrence tried to capture her hand and hold it close, but she yanked it away.

"No. You no longer have the right to call me Nessa." She paused for a moment. "Or even Vanessa. It's Miss Gailbraith to you. If I decide to let you speak to me in the future."

"Why don't you tell me what this is all about?" Lawrence, Isaac noted while smothering a laugh, was wise enough not to use any name at all in that question.

"I'm not entirely sure, but the gist of what I can figure out is that you lied to me to make me think Isaac and Clementine were engaged. And you did it so I'd say yes to your proposal."

"What?" Isaac couldn't prevent a strangled yelp.

"Shh." Julia and Mrs. MacLean hushed him immediately, but Isaac was through standing back.

"You did, didn't you?" Clementine, her hair rippling down her back, looking more rumpled than Isaac had ever seen her, was practically quivering in indignation. "How could you use me like that, Larry? I'm your sister!" She ended on a shriek.

"I knew something wasn't right." Michael crowed in triumph until Julia nudged him with her elbow.

"Is this true?" Isaac kept his voice low and calm as he came to stand beside Nessa, placing his hand at the small of her back. "I figured I didn't like you because you had your eye on Nessa, but there's more to it than that, isn't there? You have no honor."

"Don't you insult me, Isaac Freimont." Lawrence's chest puffed out in agitation. "You can't blame me for being the smarter man and seeing what a treasure Nessa—" He broke off when Nessa raised her finger. "Er, Miss Gailbraith is. I knew the moment I saw her, and she's been under your nose for your whole life. I was just man enough to step forward."

"Real men don't lie," Nessa growled. "You knew I had feelings for Isaac, and you used them to hurt me!"

"You have feelings for me?" Isaac stopped glaring at

Lawrence to look down at Nessa. "What type of feelings?"

"Don't distract me." She swatted his arm. "I'm busy telling Mr. Hepplewhite that I wouldn't marry him now if he were the last man in Montana."

"He's not," Isaac swiftly pointed out. "I'm still there."

"Why did I think we were in Wyoming right now?" Clementine sounded genuinely worried.

"We are," Mrs. MacLean assured her. "Don't worry."

"You can't blame a man for trying." Lawrence gave Nessa a look of longing that made Isaac's temper boil.

"Yes, I can." His fist clenched, Isaac stepped forward.

"Don't!" Nessa stopped him. "All I want is for him to admit what he did—own up to it."

"Yes, I tricked you." Lawrence began to look petulant. "But not for long enough." That statement had Isaac taking another step toward him, and the smaller man hastily added, "It was wrong of me. But when I overheard Isaac tell Michael he was going to break things off with Clementine, I knew I'd have to act fast. Can you forgive me for an act of desperation?"

"No." Isaac shook his head so hard he saw spots.

"Not yet," Nessa amended. "That will take time, at the very least. We don't know how much of the damage you caused can be fixed."

"Fixed?" Isaac put his hands around Nessa's waist. "So you figured out that I was talking about the time I proposed to you?"

"Yes." She gave a small smile. "That's what I meant."

"So you'll be my wife?" He grinned.

"I didn't say that. We still have some things to work out."

twenty-four

"Like what?" he demanded.

The disgruntled expression on his face made Nessa want to laugh and kiss him at the same time. "You never courted me, for one." She twinkled up at him. "The rest should fall into place after that."

"I didn't think I had to court you," he grumbled. "You were already supposed to love me."

"I do."

"Then what's the hold up? You want poems? Fancy words? Freshly picked flowers? That's all courting is."

"No, it's not." She sighed. "Courting isn't just about making the woman fall in love with you, you know."

"What else is it for?" He looked around the room, obviously hoping someone would take pity on him.

"To show the woman you love her," Julia burst out. She may even have mumbled "blockhead" under her breath, but Isaac either didn't hear it or disregarded it.

"You mean you don't already know that I love you?" He looked genuinely confused, but that didn't stop her from pushing away.

"How would I know it when you didn't even know it?" Nessa demanded. "You didn't say a word about love when you proposed!" If her finger hadn't been all achy from jabbing Lawrence, Isaac would've felt her displeasure.

"You're right." His astonished admission eased some of her temper. "I didn't know it then. I should have, but I didn't."

He spoke as though the whole thing were an incredible revelation.

"Men!" Nessa harrumphed, including both Lawrence and Isaac in that miserable category. She noticed all the women nodding and felt marginally better. "Even when I told you I cared for you, you didn't say you cared for me. That's important." She tilted her head back to scowl at him.

His smile was deeply offensive until he cupped her face in his hands, lowered his head, and touched his lips to hers. For a moment, she forgot why she'd been so riled, but then she had no choice but to wrap her arms around his neck. Otherwise, she would surely have melted into a puddle on the floor.

"Nessa?" He spoke her name softly after he drew back.

"Hmm?" She still hadn't quite recovered from his kiss.

"I love you." He whispered it in her ear, but from the whoops and hollers coming from everyone but Lawrence, nobody missed it.

"Well," Nessa told him, "it's about time."

❧

"Who's riding with Lawrence and Clementine?" Isaac glanced over to where the siblings stood by their vehicle.

"I want to stay with you." Nessa gave him a look that made Isaac want to tuck her in the car, hop in beside her, and leave everyone else behind. Not that this was possible.

"Whichever car Julia rides in, I'll be beside her." Michael took her hand in his with a questioning glance."

"I'll stay with Lawrence," Mrs. MacLean volunteered.

"Are you sure?" Julia looked vaguely guilty. "Clementine can talk a blue streak."

"Oh, so can I." The older woman laughed. "And I'd say Lawrence needs a good, long lecture after what he tried to pull. I'll enjoy giving it to him."

"I almost feel sorry for him," Nessa giggled. "Almost."

With that, they all took their places and were off. About four miles after the Roosevelt Lodge, they arrived at Crescent Hill, which stood west of the road. It didn't look much more impressive than any of the other hills, so Isaac asked Nessa why it was marked as an attraction.

"Hold on, let me read it." She squinted at the paper as they drove past, giving an outraged gasp as she read. "You'll never believe what this horrible man named Truman Everts did."

"What?" Julia perked up at the promise of a good tale.

"In 1885 he was part of the Washburn expedition—you know, the one that found the black mud hole they named the Devil's Inkpot?" She waited for their agreement before she continued. "He was fifty-seven years old, and most of the area was frozen, but he decided to head off on his own."

"That can't be good," Isaac commented. He reflected that Nessa's way of telling a story was far more interesting than Clementine's had ever been.

"No, it wasn't. He never came back. The expedition searched high and low for him but eventually was forced to move on or risk running out of supplies. Everyone figured Everts had to be dead by that time and informed his family of the tragedy."

"I don't see how that makes him a horrible man," Michael protested. "A foolish one, certainly, but not a horrible one."

"What a sad thing to have happen." Julia sounded upset.

"Oh, I'm not done yet." Nessa kept on, using a very dramatic tone. "The family was heartbroken and hired an explorer to go back to the dangerous, isolated area to find Everts's body. He was supposed to bring it back for burial, at which point he would receive a substantial reward."

"So he should, for taking on a job like that." Isaac slowed the car as they came near Hellroaring Creek.

"Well, the man found Everts, who'd been lost for thirty-seven days. And, to everybody's surprise, he'd survived. He'd lost an incredible amount of weight and was practically at death's door, crawling on the ground without any idea of where he was."

"How horrible," Julia remarked, quickly adding, "but wonderful he was rescued."

"When he got home, he refused to give the man the reward, saying that the job had been to bring home his dead body, which his rescuer certainly hadn't done." Nessa's voice rang with disgust. "Can you believe it? That's the thanks the man got for rescuing Truman Everts."

"He was horrible." Michael pounded his fist on the back of Isaac's seat. "It might have been better for everyone involved if he'd just been found dead."

"Michael!" Julia's remonstrance had the desired effect.

"Sorry, that is too harsh. Every life is precious to God," Michael amended. "It's not for me to judge."

"All the same, that was a terrible thing to do," Isaac couldn't help but say. "Maybe he's distantly related to Lawrence."

"Isaac!" Nessa gave him a light shove. "Lawrence did an awful thing, but he didn't succeed. Isn't that what really matters?"

"Yes, to us, anyway." Isaac took his eyes off the road just long enough to smile at Nessa. "That's the most important thing in the world."

twenty-five

"He proposed! Michael proposed!" Julia barely waited for Nessa to put down the bucket she'd been using to slop the pigs before grabbing her in a tight hug. They hopped and hugged and squealed together until the pigs joined in with the loud squeals of their own.

"Tell me all about it." Nessa dragged her friend away from the pigs and into the flower garden. "Every detail."

"You know he'd already asked my father for his blessing," Julia began. "So he came in the evening and asked me to go for a walk. He held my hand and took me to that little old wooden bridge over the stream by the meadow."

"In the moonlight?" Nessa sighed. "That's so romantic."

"Isn't it?" Julia couldn't stop beaming. "And under the stars, he looked into my eyes and told me he'd composed a poem. And then he looked away and said it had been so horrible he burned it. Claimed it was a stroke of mercy for us both that he couldn't even remember it."

"He's probably right." Nessa couldn't resist saying it.

"I still would have liked to hear it." Julia shrugged. "No matter how bad it was."

"Get back to the proposal itself, won't you?"

"So he sank down to one knee, never letting go of my hand, and he asked me to be his wife. 'Julia,' he said, 'by now you must know how deeply I respect you, and that the trip to Yellowstone would never have been half as enjoyable without you by my side. I've wanted to marry you for a while now, but until recently I wasn't sure if you returned the love I felt for you. Now I can only hope that you'll do me the honor of becoming my wife.'"

"And you accepted him, right?" Nessa waggled her brows. "Did he kiss you?"

"Yes, and yes." Julia laughed. "That's all the detail you're going to get though. I just couldn't wait until I could tell you this morning. Besides, I wanted to ask you something."

"I hope you're thinking about a double wedding." Nessa knew by her friend's smile that she was right. "That'll be perfect! Isaac and me pledging to love each other forever at the same ceremony where you and Michael do the same—what could be better?"

"Nothing I can imagine," her friend said with a laugh. "Can you believe that two months ago you were the one running to my house to tell me about Isaac's proposal?"

"What a difference two months make." Nessa shook her head. "If you'd asked me then, I'd have said Isaac and I would never marry. Not if that's what he wanted from a wife."

"But things have changed. Now we're planning a double wedding!" Julia gave her another hug. "It'll be in the church, of course. Michael and I will go after you and Isaac, since your engagement came first. Mama wants me to wear her wedding dress, but I'll have to let out the hem first. I'm a good four inches taller than she is."

"I'll probably wear my ma's gown, too," Nessa confessed. "Though I'll need to modify it a little bit, because I don't wear corsets."

"With your tiny waist, you won't need to do much. Saturday, let's get together and work on our dresses." Julia grabbed Nessa's hands. "The wedding could take place the week after, unless you think folks would be scandalized."

"I doubt it. Everyone's been expecting this since we returned from Yellowstone and the Hepplewhites packed up," her friend assured her. "No one's ever left Saddleback so quickly, but the new family that bought their land seems nice."

"After my last error in judgment, I think I'll wait until they've been around for a while before I agree with you." Nessa smoothed her skirts. "For now, we both have a lot of things to do. We can't leave our families with a lot of work piled up."

"All right. I'll see you later—to plan for our wedding!"

❧

"So you did it, then?" Isaac didn't really even need to ask. His friend's face told him everything he needed to know.

"She said yes." Michael flopped down onto the soft but scratchy hay. "Didn't even have to think twice, just promised to join her life with mine as though she couldn't imagine saying no. I'm the luckiest man in the world, Isaac. Couldn't ask for a better woman than my Julia."

"That's right." Isaac gave him a friendly punch to the shoulder. "But only because Nessa's taken."

"I should have known you'd try to claim something like that." Michael shook his head. "I suppose the wisest thing would be to let you continue on in your way of thinking."

"When have you ever done the wisest thing?"

"A good bit more often than you, my friend." Michael lobbed a fistful of hay at him. "Which is why I'm going to say you have the best woman for you and I have the best woman for me. Beyond that, we're both entitled to our separate opinions."

"Even if you're wrong," Isaac promptly agreed.

"You're lucky I'm in such a good mood, or I'd have to make you take that back." Michael gave a contented sigh. "As it is, nothing can detract from the beauty of this day."

"Oh brother." Isaac rolled his eyes. "You're not going to wax poetic, are you?"

"No." Michael seemed oddly flushed. "I've learned I don't have the talent for it, so I'll leave it to men who don't actually have wives to keep them busy."

"You don't have a wife yet," Isaac pointed out. "Not that you'll be single much longer."

"Don't want to be." His friend pillowed his head on his hands, staring up at the roof of the barn. "Julia's supposed to talk with Nessa today, see if she'd mind having a double wedding."

"So you don't think you need to ask if I'd mind?" Isaac pretended to be insulted. "You take a lot for granted."

"What? I brought it up now, didn't I?" Michael bit back a laugh. "Not that it'll make much of a difference what you think once Nessa's all excited about sharing her wedding with her best friend."

"That's true." He chewed reflexively on a piece of hay. "There isn't much I'd deny Nessa if it'd make her smile."

"Now who's waxing poetic?"

"Watch what you say. I don't want to disappoint Julia by having you injured." Isaac stretched. "Besides, Nessa wouldn't like it if I 'accidentally' rolled you out of this hayloft and you sprained something."

"Does she know how violent you are?" Michael raised his brows. "She should be warned that you threaten other men."

"Only men who stand between me and my bride-to-be."

"Still itching a little over not having a man-to-man with Lawrence before he hightailed it?" Michael knew him very well.

"A little," he admitted. "Though it's not what God would have wanted, so it's a blessing the Hepplewhites packed up.

I wasn't entirely sure I was ready to turn the other cheek after what Lawrence did."

"Can't say I blame you, but we're called to be stronger than we'd ever manage on our own."

"Think that's why God gave us such incredible women?" Isaac wondered aloud. "He knew we'd need extra help to become the men He had in mind?"

"I'd believe that's part of it." Michael rolled onto his side. "But I'd say a bigger part is His grace in giving us a reward we don't deserve. The sooner we get our women down the aisle, the better."

"Afraid Julia might realize she made a mistake?" Isaac scooted out of the way before Michael could grab him. "Hey, that was a joke. Won't happen again, I promise."

"It better not." Michael sat back down. "How long do you think it's going to take for us to become settled-down husbands, stuck in a rut we refuse to climb out of?"

"One of two ways," Isaac considered. "Either as soon as we're married and we have everything we ever wanted, or. . ."

"Or what?"

"Or it'll take Nessa and Julia an eternity to whip us into the husbands they deserve." Isaac grinned. "Is it wrong that I'm kind of hoping it'll be the second one?"

"Probably." Michael laughed. "But I hope so, too. I want every minute I can get with my wife-to-be."

"My thoughts, exactly."

twenty-six

"Can I look yet?" Nessa fidgeted in the chair while Julia gave her hair a trim. "Please let me look. I know it's perfect."

"If you know it's perfect, then you don't need to look." Julia gave another judicious snip with the scissors.

"That's only because today everything will be perfect." Nessa paused and added as an afterthought, "Even if everything isn't, it'll seem that way to me."

"I know what you mean." Julia put down the scissors and held up the looking glass. "Now you can see."

"It is perfect!" Nessa fingered the newly trimmed tendrils framing her face and peered at the freckles barely discernible beneath a translucent layer of pressed powder. "In the real way, not the it's-my-wedding-so-it-has-to-be way," she clarified. "And our hairstyles even match!"

"I saw how much you liked mine, so I thought it would be a nice touch for our double wedding." Julia turned the looking glass and surveyed her profile to see the elegant sweep of curls falling from a simple twist high atop her head. "It is a pretty style, if the pins stay in."

Nessa admired her friend's willowy figure. "If you didn't say so, no one would know you were wearing your mother's dress. The lace you added to the bottom looks so sophisticated."

"Even if I hadn't mentioned it, everyone would still know, since Mama has told anyone who will listen." Julia bit her lip. "Do you think Michael will like it?"

"He'd have to be a fool not to, and we both know he's no

fool." Nessa fingered the soft cream satin of her own wedding gown. "After all, he knows to marry you!"

"That's true. Have I told you how wonderful you look in your mother's dress?" Julia asked. "When you walk, it seems like you're floating on a whispering cloud."

"You have such a way with words." Nessa couldn't help but be pleased in spite of herself. "Julia, there's no one in the world I'd rather share this special day with."

"Except Isaac, of course."

"It wouldn't be a special day without Isaac." Nessa affixed her veil while Julia did the same, finishing right as a knock sounded on the door. She hurried to open it. "Da!" Nessa relished his big hug as John Mathers went to embrace Julia. She noticed that her friend was having a soft conversation with her own father, so she was able to concentrate fully on the man who'd loved and raised her.

"'Tis time," he rumbled. "Are you both ready to meet your fortunate grooms? Ach, anyone with a pair of eyes could see you're more than ready. Such a lovely set of brides I've never seen." He held out his hand, and Nessa took it.

"When have you ever seen a set of brides?" she teased. "I didn't know you'd ever attended another double wedding."

"Don't think your old da can't see what you're up to, Nessa." He shook his head. "Nothing you say will make it easy for me to give you away, not even to the man you love."

"Oh, Da." Nessa rose on her tiptoes to kiss his cheek. "We're staying in Saddleback, so it's not as though you'll even have time to miss me!" In spite of the light words, tears sprang to her eyes. There was something bittersweet about leaving her family behind, even to be with the man she loved.

"Are we ready to go?" Mr. Mathers escorted Julia outside.

When both girls had carefully arranged the fragile skirts of their wedding gowns, the men closed the car doors and drove them the short distance to the church. In no time at all, Nessa stood beside her father before the double doors.

"I love you, Da," She whispered. "That'll never change."

"You'll always be my Nessa"—he patted her arm—"even after I give you away. You remember that you're not leaving us behind. We're happy to see you move forward. Are you ready?"

"Yes, Da." Nessa straightened her shoulders. "I'm ready."

≈

This is it. She's probably right outside those doors, Isaac told himself as Alma struck up a processional on the piano. She's arranging those gauzy things women wear at weddings, taking her father's arm, and starting to walk down the aisle now. He blinked and opened his eyes, hoping to see her appear. She didn't.

Any minute now, he revised. Aaannnyyy minute. He wiped a bead of sweat from his brow as the doors stayed closed. *She wouldn't come to her senses and realize she deserves better than me now, right, Lord? Not on the day of our wedding. I promise I'll be the best husband I can possibly be, if only Nessa marries me today. . .*

The doors opened to reveal Nessa, escorted down the aisle by her father. Ewan Gailbraith may have been a big, burly blacksmith, but Isaac could only see his bride as she breezed down the aisle, a vision in white. *Thank You, Lord.*

When she reached him, she gave a smile so bright that it couldn't be hidden beneath her veil. Isaac eagerly accepted her hand as Ewan formally gave away the bride. He reveled in the warmth of her soft grip as Julia made her way down the aisle and Michael sucked in a sharp breath, much the way Isaac had when he'd seen Nessa.

In the blink of an eye, all four of them stood before the

pastor, ready to be wed. The man of God welcomed everyone to the joyous occasion, and the ceremony began in earnest.

"Before I begin, there is a request I must fulfill." The pastor unfolded the sheet of paper Isaac had slipped him that morning. "The grooms have asked that I read this quote and promise before the vows are exchanged."

Isaac nodded as Nessa tilted her head in silent question. She looked ahead as the pastor began to read.

"A famous man once said, 'Love does not consist in gazing at each other but in looking together in the same direction.' Isaac and Michael both wanted Vanessa and Julia to know that, though they'll find it difficult to look away from the beauty of their wives, they're blessed to have found women who will look to God to guide them through marriage."

Nessa gave Isaac's hand a tight squeeze, and he squeezed back.

The next few minutes passed in a blur of "I do's" as Isaac and Nessa, then Michael and Julia repeated their vows. Isaac slowly drew off Nessa's white glove, sliding a gold band onto her left ring finger. He didn't pay attention to the others, but Michael must have done the same for Julia.

"I now pronounce you man and wife," the pastor proclaimed. "You may each kiss your bride."

Isaac didn't need any further invitation. He lifted the gauzy fabric concealing her face, tossing it away. Then he batted it back as it fell improperly. Then he gathered her in his arms, tilted her back, and gave her a kiss filled with all the promise of his love.

When he straightened up, her lips were rosy from contact with his, her eyes sparkling with tears. She opened her mouth and laughed.

The joyous sound was irresistible, and Isaac found himself

joining in with chuckles of his own as he held her hand in his and took her up the aisle.

"This," he told her after they'd left the church, "is the first day of our life together and the beginning of the joy and laughter we'll share."

"I love you, Isaac Freimont." She leaned forward to brush her lips against his. When she moved to draw away, he pulled her back.

"I love you, too, Nessa Freimont."

"Isaac?" she murmured after their next kiss. "I was right."

"About what?"

"I finally caught you."

epilogue

Montana, 1920

"I'd say our family reunion has officially outgrown our home," Dustin Freimont told his wife, who nestled so sweetly at his side. "What do you think?"

"The Lord has blessed us beyond what we ever could have hoped for." Delana surveyed her family with obvious satisfaction.

Brent, Marlene, and Isaac all had their spouses and children present. The Gailbraiths and Horntons, joined by happy marriages, mingled with everyone. Delana's old friend, Kaitlin MacLean, sat with a blanket over her lap, surrounded by children.

"I never would have thought God would see fit to give us so many loved ones. Or that the spread I was so focused on proving up would be the beginning of an entire town." Dustin leaned back. "We've seen so many good years under the Montana sky."

"And so much growth." Delana took a sip of water. "From covered wagons, to the railroad, to private automobiles, Saddleback has kept pace with progress."

"I'd say we stayed ahead of the curve." Dustin gave a groan as he got to his feet then reached to pull his wife up beside him. "Because we always had the one thing technology could never improve upon."

"Love," she agreed, resting her head against his chest.

Her golden hair had faded to white, her skin held the lines of laughter, and his wife was more beautiful to him than on the day they'd met. "Love," he agreed, looking out on the many blessings of God's love and the love shared among their family. "And time."

" 'To every thing,' " his wife began, " 'there is a season.' "

" 'And a time to every purpose under the heaven,' " he joined her. " 'A time to be born, and a time to die; a time to plant, and a time to pluck up that which is planted; a time to kill, and a time to heal; a time to break down, and a time to build up; a time to weep,' "—he looked into her eyes, seeing his own happiness mirrored there—" 'and a time to laugh. . . .' "

A Letter To Our Readers

Dear Reader:

In order that we might better contribute to your reading enjoyment, we would appreciate your taking a few minutes to respond to the following questions. We welcome your comments and read each form and letter we receive. When completed, please return to the following:

Fiction Editor
Heartsong Presents
PO Box 719
Uhrichsville, Ohio 44683

1. Did you enjoy reading *A Time to Laugh* by Kelly Eileen Hake?
   ❏ Very much! I would like to see more books by this author!
   ❏ Moderately. I would have enjoyed it more if

   _____

   _____

   _____

2. Are you a member of **Heartsong Presents**? ❏ Yes ❏ No
   If no, where did you purchase this book? _____

   _____

3. How would you rate, on a scale from 1 (poor) to 5 (superior), the cover design? _____

4. On a scale from 1 (poor) to 10 (superior), please rate the following elements.

   ____ Heroine   ____ Plot
   ____ Hero   ____ Inspirational theme
   ____ Setting   ____ Secondary characters

5. These characters were special because? _____

_____

_____

6. How has this book inspired your life? _____

_____

_____

7. What settings would you like to see covered in future **Heartsong Presents** books? _____

_____

_____

8. What are some inspirational themes you would like to see treated in future books? _____

_____

_____

9. Would you be interested in reading other **Heartsong Presents** titles? ❏ Yes ❏ No

10. Please check your age range:

❏ Under 18   ❏ 18-24

❏ 25-34   ❏ 35-45

❏ 46-55   ❏ Over 55

Name_____

Occupation _____

Address _____

City, State, Zip_____

Hearts❤ng

HISTORICAL ROMANCE IS CHEAPER BY THE DOZEN!

Buy any assortment of twelve *Heartsong Presents* titles and save 25% off of the already discounted price of $2.97 each!

HEARTSONG PRESENTS TITLES AVAILABLE NOW:

(If ordering from this page, please remember to include it with the order form.)

Presents